Nana had refused to let go of her son, Lou, for as long as she was alive. Only death had managed to pry loose her smothering, maternal grip. Now that she was finally gone, Gloria wanted her mother-in-law to stay dead.

Not for her to be approaching down the hallway...

IN THE VICTORIAN TRADITION

Christmas Ghost Story is the literary descendant of the traditional British ghost stories told by family and friends around the Christmas Eve hearth.

Charles Dickens, whose *A Christmas Carol* was among the most popular Victorian ghost stories, was also one of the form's most active enthusiasts. He edited and published two magazines, and urged his contemporary literary giants to contribute supernatural thrillers. Soon all the best magazines were putting out special bulky Christmas issues with chilling supernatural tales by the literary names of the day.

This novel is a revival of that Victorian tradition, a Christmas ghost story set in the Pacific Northwest of the 1990's.

Christmas
Ghost Story

by

Nick DiMartino

ROSEBRIAR PUBLISHING
Lynnwood, Washington

Christmas Ghost Story

Rosebriar Publishing
820 195th Place S.W.
Lynnwood, Washington 98036
(206) 776-3865

ISBN 0-9653918-0-9

Library of Congress cataloguing-in-publication data is available.

for my family,
with love

in memory of a very dear friend
John Kauffman

Special thanks to
Jolene Lennon, rock of faith; Robert Carlberg, storyline technician;
Kent and Jena Schliiter, logic hounds; Diane Mapes, beloved slasher;
Sherry Laing, faithful critic; Greg DiMartino, wish-maker; and
Jim Latteier, Lori Morgan, Geoff and Emilyn Wright, Judith Chandler,
Kay Story, Henry Jenkins, Pamela Harlow, Mark Hafs,
Antoinette Wills, Farrish Sharon, Liz Fugate, Carla Rickerson,
Mark Mouser, Jonathan Day, Ruth and Paul Lewing,
and all the others

Christmas Ghost Story

CHAPTER ONE

House on Maynard Street

1
The Dream

It isn't the first time, because she remembers the red roses on one side, the white roses on the other. It isn't the last time, either. She isn't afraid yet.

How old is she? Five, maybe. She looks up at the house towering over her. The walls are made of red bricks. Even the porch is made of bricks. A narrow strip of flower garden wraps nicely around it.

She runs to the end of the walkway, to the flowers. The snapdragons are in bloom, purple and blue and yellow. She wants to pinch them, to make them snap like Nana taught her, but she doesn't. Once a bee was inside when she pinched. It stung her.

She's with her Dad. She can't remember who else. Maybe her Mom is there, or else her step mother, Barbara. Dad knocks, and then opens the front door. Grandma and Grandpa are already inside, and Uncle Tony, too. Everyone is standing up and hugging everybody else as they come in the door.

She should be going inside, too. She doesn't want to leave the flowers.

And then she sees her. An old woman in a pink sweater with her hair coiled in a tight, gray bun has stepped out on the porch. She's still wearing her cooking apron, wiping her hands on a dishtowel. She's watching her play in the garden, her eyes bright, smiling, so full of love. It's Nana.

She begins to run slowly toward her great-grandmother.

Nana bends down to her level and opens her arms to embrace her.

"How's my big girl? How's my Gina?"

2
Happy Palace

Gina opened her eyes.

Nana was gone.

A pink neon castle, suspended on a neon rainbow twenty feet in the air, spilled its electric glow through the motel window. The hiss and roar of morning traffic beat at the window like surf.

Gina Rossi was twenty-two now, a recent graduate of Notre Dame. Instead of being at Nana's house, she was looking up at the pink ceiling of Room 11 in the Happy Palace Motel on Aurora Avenue. She had come back. She had spent most of her childhood in the Seattle-Tacoma area, had always thought of it as home — the home to which she was returning.

She stretched her long legs, pulling out the covers at the bottom of the motel bed. She was five-foot-nine and proud of every inch, lanky and strong and healthy. Her black curls were short, thick and shaggy. Her dark brown eyes blinked awake now, long lashes guarding the depths. Though raised in the rainy Northwest and returning from four years in Indiana, her olive skin gave her the look of a perpetual suntan.

Aaron was still asleep beside her, the blankets fallen off his bare shoulders, his face buried in his pillow, snoring softly. He was an Easterner, paler, new to the west coast, exhausted from seven days of determined apartment-hunting. Together they were looking for a place to live for the next four years while he attended medical school.

He was two inches taller than Gina, with short black hair, black eyes, a hawk nose, a perpetual stubble on a clas-

2

sic jaw. His good looks had gotten him in trouble all his life. His brains had gotten him out of it.

He was awake now, shifting, stretching. Rolling over on his side, he cuddled up next to her.

"Good morning, gorgeous." He kissed her.

She returned the kiss, but her thoughts were elsewhere. "I just had that dream again."

"Seattle seems to be good for dreaming." He snuggled up next to her. "You've been having that dream every night." He nuzzled her neck gently. "Maybe I can help you forget it."

3
U. District

It was mid-afternoon before they were actually in the car heading toward the University of Washington.

Banking down the blue-gray exit, under the bright, blue-gray sky, they came to a abrupt halt in the stop-and-go, mostly stopped, traffic at the heart of the University District. Backed up on 45th, sandwiched between a family van and a bus, they were crawling, stoplight by stoplight, toward the crowded street ahead, the colorful human jungle called the Ave.

He had been watching her face for some time, and he finally just said it. "Why don't you call them?"

"Call who?"

She had been staring out the windshield. Not at the river of students, punks, homeless and elderly bumping and jostling across the street in front of her. At something that was hurting her, something she wasn't telling him.

"Call them, and get it over with."

Aaron Steiner came from a large Jewish family in New Jersey, so he could understand the emotional chaos she was going through, even if he didn't know all the details. Family. He could love his family so much better when he was far enough away from them. There was nothing wrong with

3

family, of course. With luck — and Aaron always had luck — his family would pay for his entire medical schooling. Maybe even set him up in the family practice. But they were always getting involved in things that were none of their business. They couldn't help it.

Which was why the west coast was a good idea. His parents could pay for tuition and books, food and rent, and didn't have to know he was living with a pretty, hot-blooded Catholic girl. Ever since he had collided with Gina Rossi in his bio-chem class, she had come to mean more to him than anyone else in the world.

He started dating her two years ago, in the spring of their sophomore year, a few months before she flew home to Tacoma for the summer. They wrote back and forth. They phoned every week. Something was happening between them.

Gina's mother had married a Boeing engineer with a ten-year-old daughter of his own. One Sunday afternoon the three of them drove off to the mall, and never got there. They were suddenly snatched out of Gina's life forever, left behind on the side of the freeway in a crumpled fist of steel.

She had called him that day, incoherent with crying. He managed to postpone a summer quarter exam, dipped into next month's allowance for airfare, and caught the first flight to Seattle. She was waiting for him at Sea-Tac Airport. She sobbed in his arms. It was a turning point for both of them.

They returned to Notre Dame together after the funerals, and had been together ever since. Aaron had liked Seattle, liked the University of Washington, applied to the medical school, and been accepted. Gina came with him, back to the first city she ever thought of as home, with career plans of her own.

Now all they needed was some place that was clean, cheap, and close to campus, a place to recover each day from the rigors of medical school. A place to endure the struggle for four years, until he became Dr. Steiner and they made a final commitment to each other.

"Don't you think it's time you gave your family a call?"

4

She flinched. "What in the world brought that up?"

"It's been seven days," said Aaron. "My family would go through the ceiling if they found out I'd been in town for a whole week and not called them."

"How is my family going to find out I'm in town?"

"Families always find out," he said. "Why don't you want them to know you're in Seattle?"

"I do want them to know," insisted Gina. "Just not yet."

"I don't understand what you're waiting for." Was she ashamed to introduce him to her father? Were Catholic parents as uptight as Jewish parents?

"Maybe I'll call them tonight," she said. "Maybe not. It has to be the perfect time, Aaron. Trust me. I want things to be just exactly right when I call them. You know how important this is to me."

"Whatever you say." He reached across the seat and closed his hand over hers. "It's your decision."

4
Wrong Exit

She circled around through the University District after dropping him off. Traffic had not improved.

She glanced uneasily at her watch. She had a job interview at four o'clock with Green World Landscaping. They were looking for an experienced arborist, but were willing to consider her. She tried to compose her thoughts, to remember her good points, to concentrate on how she would present herself.

Instead, her attention kept wandering. She couldn't stop puzzling over her dream. She'd been having it every night since she came back to Seattle.

Another stoplight.

She stared through the windshield. She barely noticed the teenagers with candy-colored hair, the activists with petition boards, the homeless with bedrolls and crumpled belongings.

Out of the corner of her eye, just before the light changed, she noticed an old woman in a long black overcoat, her head wrapped in a red kerchief, clutching her small black purse, waiting at the bus-stop.

The old woman looked exactly like Nana.

With a gasp, Gina turned back for another look. A bus wheezed up to the curb, erasing the old woman from sight.

An impatient horn blared behind her. The light had changed.

Gina's foot came down heavily on the gas pedal. Her car lurched forward. She strained for one last sight of the old woman in the rear view mirror. She was so intent on spotting her that she wasn't thinking about the freeway.

Before she realized what she was doing, she had gone too far west, missed the northbound entrance altogether, and was crossing over the freeway in the left turn lane, banking southbound.

Too late to change lanes. There was only one direction. She took it.

The strange thing, she realized afterward, was that she never tried to correct her error. She didn't take the first exit off the freeway. She didn't turn around and head north to Green World Landscaping. She forgot about her interview altogether.

She simply continued driving south.

5
Woman in the Alley

She was a stranger in the neighborhood, a young woman with curly black hair that he'd never seen before, staring rudely out her car window at the back of his house.

"Excuse me," she called toward the garden. "Do you live here?"

Sokha Sok laid down his trowel and resigned himself to a pause in his weeding. His garden would have to wait. He had a guest, whether he wanted one or not.

6

"Can you help me?"

Americans asked the most amazing questions. How could he possibly know that? Perhaps he could help her, perhaps not. What was the proper way to answer such a question?

He smiled and nodded ambiguously.

The troubled young woman hadn't waited for an answer. Her car door was open, and she was striding toward his orderly green rows of tomatoes and beans and lettuce.

He sincerely hoped she wouldn't take long. Time was his most precious possession. August had already slipped through his fingers. All too soon it would be wet and cold outdoors. Being trapped inside that house all day with his unhappy wife and her complaining mother was like being sealed in a coffin.

That house!

If only someone would take that bad-luck curse off his hands. It was already almost September. The real estate agent had assured him that it would be sold by now. He absolutely refused to spend one more Christmas in that place. He refused! Even if he had to move out for the night and spend Christmas Eve in a motel room.

Straightening his back, he rose stiffly to his feet.

A weathered Panama hat protected him from the harsh rays of the late August sun. The wide straw brim hid most of his face. Black sunglasses concealed his eyes. What features were visible revealed no age. His body was lost in a bulky old sweatshirt and baggy, grass-stained pants.

"Are you looking for some place?" he asked.

"No," she said. "Not any more." She smiled.

Sokha Sok puzzled over this. Then he noticed that her eyes were wet.

"You see, I used to play here. Can you believe it? Here in this yard, and over past that garden-bed. There used to be swings on the other side of the hedge."

Her glistening eyes saw a house and a yard from a different time, gardens and fences that were no longer there.

"You came here before?"

"Long ago," she said. "When I was just a little kid."

"Little kids don't come here now," he said. "They stay away. Many years this house owned by a crazy old lady. She get too crazy to live here. Little kids play in the yard, they say crazy old lady yell at them. She scares them away with a broom. She is dead now, I think."

"Yes, she's dead," she said. "That crazy old lady was my great-grandmother."

Sokha Sok gasped. He was horrified by his own indiscreet remarks. "I am very ashamed to speak of your departed great-grandmother with such disrespect. Please forgive me."

"That's okay." She smiled. "She *was* a little crazy there at the end. Nothing you say can hurt her now."

"House for sale," he mentioned hopefully. He immediately regretted it. Another indiscretion.

The mysterious young woman looked at him. Then she shielded her eyes from the sun with her hand, and stared up at the house, as though listening to something he couldn't hear.

Sokha Sok wondered if she already suspected. Something was wrong with that house, very wrong. How often he had watched cousins or in-laws, newly-arrived from Cambodia, storm downstairs in the middle of the night and move into motels! He told her nothing. He knew enough English to make himself understood, but what could he say? That the house was haunted? Such things were not admitted in America. How could he confess that the house had brought him and his family nothing but frustration and alarm and occasionally terror for three years?

He had scarcely slept for the last three nights. Once again, it was starting to get worse. And if it was bad now, at the end of August, think how it would be closer to Christmas! It always got worse at Christmas.

He could feel the house leaning over him now. He tried to concentrate on uprooting weeds. He waited for her to leave. She didn't leave.

"The house is no longer for sale," she said. "I've decided to buy it."

6
Mantra

Aaron was hot and sweaty as he got off the bus on Aurora Avenue. He was dripping wet by the time he walked the two remaining blocks to the Happy Palace, his backpack bulging with heavy, expensive new textbooks. With a clattering of the plastic motel key, he elbowed his way through the doorway, juggling three white boxes of Chinese take-out.

He was about to announce, "Your Highness is served!" Instead he simply stopped in the doorway.

Gina was pacing back and forth, talking to herself excitedly, as though she had gone completely crazy. She had kicked off her shoes. Her hair was tossled, her cheeks flushed. Newspapers were scattered all over the floor from their daily apartment-hunting. There she was in the middle of them, like some barefoot medieval penitent, pacing from one wall of the motel room to the other, repeating, "Oh my God oh my God oh my God oh my God oh my God—!"

He cleared his throat.

She looked up and screamed. "Aaron!" He just managed to set down the boxes of Chinese food before she was in his arms.

"Good job interview?" he guessed.

She didn't hear him. She was shouting out her news in such excitement, in such confusion, that all he deciphered was his own name, periodically, and an address repeated like the chanting of a mantra, "1716 South Maynard Street."

"Is it really that great?" he squeezed in edgewise, as he slung his heavy backpack to the floor.

"It's the best," she said. "The very best."

"You've checked it out? It's available?"

"Better. It's ours."

He stared at her. "Ours? What do you mean? You made a down payment?"

"Aaron, it's our house. I've found it. I've found our house."

9

"A house? Are you sure we can afford a house?"

Her cheeks were flushed. "It's the house in my dream."

"You've rented it? Without me even seeing it?"

"Oh, my God, you're right," she said. "You're absolutely right. You have to see it. Right now." She slipped into her shoes, grabbed the keys off the motel bed. "Let's go."

"Hey, slow down!" he cried, chasing after her. "So, are we celebrating? Was the interview a success? Am I sharing this house with a breadwinner?"

She gasped. "Green World! I totally forgot about it."

"You forgot about your job interview?" But she was heading out the door. "Hey, what about dinner?" He gestured toward the greasy cartons, which he had transported by bus all the way from campus. "Barbecued pork. Deluxe chow mien. Almond chicken."

She didn't hear him.

7
Facing the Landlady

"So, tell me again, why exactly are you in love with it?"

He looked up at the house. An old brick monstrosity in a tired, declining neighborhood, unwieldy, troublesome, drafty, probably cost a fortune to heat in the winter, and much too far from campus. This was the house of her dreams?

"You don't love it?" She sounded genuinely surprised. "You don't think it's the perfect place to start a new life? Come on, admit it. You love it. Don't tease me."

"Not love," he said. He smiled reassuringly, trying to be a good sport. "But possibly *like*. A very qualified like." He squinted up at the unfriendly brick walls. The current owner was nowhere in sight, though Aaron noticed a curtain move in the kitchen window. "So, break the news to me. How much do we pay a month for this dump?"

"Dump?" She scowled at him. "Nothing, Aaron. We won't be paying rent."

"No rent?" He looked at her quizzically. "Who's letting us stay here for free?"

She looked up at the house. "Not free. Your share will be three hundred a month, utilities included, the amount you agreed to pay for an apartment."

"My share? What do you mean, my share? Do I assume your share is the same?"

"I don't have a share. It's mine. I'm buying it."

Aaron took a step backward. "I can't be hearing right. You're buying a house?" His smile crumpled. He was no longer being witty.

She shrugged her shoulders, at a loss to explain. "It was for sale, and there I was, and—"

"This has to be a joke." He didn't find it funny. "I thought we were looking for a place to rent, just long enough for me to finish—"

"I know, I know," said Gina, throwing her arms around his neck, kissing him impatiently to silence him. "But that was before I knew."

He pulled away from her lips enough to say, "Knew what?"

"Knew that we could have Nana's house."

"I don't understand a word you're saying."

"My great-grandmother lived here, Aaron. This is where Grandpa grew up. It's a major landmark of my childhood. It was always a part of our family, the place where everybody went at Christmas. I loved this old house. And then it was sold after she died, and all of a sudden I've been dreaming about this house, for no reason. The same dream, over and over. And then I accidentally get on the freeway going the wrong way, and before I know it I'm here in real life and it's for sale. I mean, what am I supposed to think?"

He looked at her blankly. "What do you think?"

"I think I've upset you, haven't I?" She hugged him. "I'm sorry. I didn't mean to."

"Gina, I'm going to be honest with you." He pulled away enough to look her in the eye. She had a look that Aaron recognized, but couldn't quite place. "You're going a little fast for me. You've got to slow down. Just when I'm getting

11

comfortable with you, feeling like I know you, you casually make a major decision without even asking my opinion. You just happen to buy a house, on the spur of the moment. Our agreement was to rent a place until I graduate. I never agreed to buy a house!"

"You aren't buying the house," she said quietly. "I am. It'll take most of my mother's insurance money. I'm absolutely certain it's the right decision."

In that instant, Aaron realized where he'd seen that look in her eyes. First thing in the morning, after one of her dreams.

She put her hands on her hips. "From now on, Mr. Steiner, you will consider me your landlady. You'll be expected to pay your rent on the first of the month, without fail. No pets. No loud music. No parties. No girls."

"No girls?"

"Well, maybe one girl. But only one." She kissed him. "For special tenants, the landlady grants certain favors."

"Favors?"

She kissed him. "Lots of favors."

His resistance collapsed. "I surrender all tenant rights," he murmured in her ear. "When can I move in?"

CHAPTER TWO

Family Trouble

1
A Shock at the Triplex

Chilly, deceptive September sun streamed through the second-floor picture window.

The cold light illuminated a cozy, well-kept living room, every surface free of dust and adorned with photographs. Grandchildren at every age and stage of development were framed and mounted on end tables, coffee table, hearthstone and mantelpiece, under the lamps and on top of the television. Though there were only three grandchildren, there appeared to be a stadium full of them.

The excited commentary of a sports announcer filled the room, accompanying a broad-shouldered, helmeted black athlete battering his way down a crowded football field, hurtling straight toward the television screen, toward the sunlit living room of Lou and Gloria Rossi.

Far from Beacon Hill, the old neighborhood in south Seattle where they had raised their two sons, the Rossis were now happily settled in the upper unit of a sturdy, modern triplex in safer, saner north Seattle, where their grandchildren were within easy driving distance and their neighbors spoke English.

Lou Rossi sat in his favorite chair, feet up on the hassock, the Saturday newspaper spread open across his Bermuda shorts. He was a healthy, sun-browned man in his seventies, and had paused in his newspaper-reading long enough to notice the scores on the television screen.

The ringing of the telephone jolted him back from the football field.

"Hello?"

He didn't recognize the voice, couldn't hear exactly what the woman was saying.

"Can you speak up?"

The connection was terrible. Or was it the football game? Where was the remote control?

"—Grandpa."

And then he knew. It was the precious granddaughter he hadn't seen for two years, not since her mother's funeral, not since she had departed from Sea-Tac Airport returning to her college in Indiana. "Is this Gina?"

He finally found the remote control, but it only made the football crowd roar louder. It didn't matter. He knew who was calling now.

"Gina, it's you!" he said. "Your Grandma will be so upset that she missed your call. She just drove to the supermarket to pick up a few things. How's Indiana?"

She said something.

He made her say it again. "Here?" Could she possibly be here? Already in Seattle? "Where are you calling from, Gina? Are you at the airport? Do you need a ride?"

But she wasn't at the airport. She didn't need a ride. She had a lot to tell him. A lot.

2
"Is It Your Heart?"

When Gloria Rossi got home from the supermarket, she carried two full grocery bags up the twelve cement stairs through the front garden, then up the ten wood-and-steel stairs to the front door (which she nudged and bumped open), and then up the fourteen carpeted inside stairs of the triplex to the second floor.

That was a lot of stairs, whether you were seventy-two years old or not.

Gloria prided herself on not being out of breath. She was as lean and sun-browned as her husband. She played golf three times a week and took daily morning walks with Lou around Green Lake. She wore her thick, gray hair in a short-cropped helmet. She regarded life from a skeptical, cautious stance. Gloria was a trim, compact woman who walked straight and said what she thought.

She was mildly surprised that her husband didn't meet her at the door and take the grocery bags from her arms. That would have been more like him. She juggled the bulging bags, fumbled her key into the lock, and pushed the door open with her foot.

"Lou? Can you give me a hand?" she called from the doorway. Her words crackled with irritation. She could hear the television in the front room. The game was on. The world stopped when the game was on.

"Lou?"

She scowled, adjusted the weight of the bulky bags in her arms, and rapidly walked to the end of the hall.

"Lou—?"

She strode into the kitchen, and was about to call again when she saw him sitting in one of the kitchen chairs, staring at the floor. The telephone receiver was in one hand, wailing indignantly, demanding to be disconnected.

The sight unhinged her.

She worried constantly about her husband's weight, his diet, his cholesterol level. She hounded him over his shameless taste for red meat. Now she took one look at him, overturned her bags onto the spotless counter, rushed to her husband, seized him.

"Lou!"

"Huh? What?"

"Where does it hurt?"

"I'm okay. Really."

"What is it? Lou, tell me. Is it your heart?"

Because if it was Lou's heart, it was Gloria's heart, too. She had already decided years ago that if Lou died first, she would follow him immediately, regardless of what anyone said, by any means necessary.

The thought of losing her husband always brought a strange and terrible image to mind. It was a commonly told story in the Rossi family that during the first year after her husband's death, Nana had walked to the bus stop on Beacon Avenue every morning like clockwork. She always caught the same bus, always fulfilled the same ritual, riding into downtown Seattle, where she transferred to another bus that carried her north to Calvary Cemetery. There Orsola Rossi would throw herself sobbing on the grave of her husband, pound the earth with her fists, and beg God to take her, too.

Gloria could imagine that kind of pain.

She wrapped a supporting arm around her husband's shoulders. "Can you stand up?"

"I don't want to stand up," said Lou. "I want to stay right here." He sighed. "We just got a call from Gina."

"From Notre Dame?"

"She's back."

Her face brightened into grandmotherly bliss. "How wonderful!"

"She's going to live here in Seattle."

"Live here!" Gloria burst into delighted laughter. "What terrific news! Lou, you scared the hell out of me. What's wrong with you? You look like you just heard the worst—"

"She'll be living with her boyfriend."

"Oh, no." Her smile crumpled. "How unfortunate. How disappointing. I always hoped Gina would have more sense. Oh, well. Some nice young lawyer from Notre Dame."

"He's Jewish."

"Jewish? Not the one we met two years ago, when Gina's mother—?"

"That's him."

"Oh, my. Why do young people have to make things so difficult? Two different religions! Oh, well. If he makes a good husband."

"They have no plans to get married. And she said not to worry. She's being safe. She's on the pill."

"The pill—"

Gloria felt dizzy. Her granddaughter was still a child!

16

She was thoroughly depressed before Lou even got to the end of the bad news list.

"And Gina is using her inheritance and the money from the insurance to buy my mother's old place."

"What? What?"

"Nana's house," he said to his wife. "Our granddaughter plans to buy Nana's house."

The very thought of Nana's house was enough to cause Gloria's knees to give out. If there was one place she'd had enough of for the rest of her life, it was Nana's house.

She dropped onto a kitchen chair beside her husband. "Has she told her father yet?"

"Of course not," he said.

"Lou, don't get involved," she warned. "You know what our son can be like."

"We're keeping out of it," said Lou. "I'll help her close the deal. I'll help her with the paperwork. But I won't help her when it comes to Sam. I don't meddle in my son's affairs. It's up to Gina to tell her father about her living arrangements. Not us."

3
The View from the 29th Floor

Gusts of rain lashed at the wall-size windows, high above the darkening streets of downtown Seattle. Wobbly, glistening raindrop trails streaked the glass, blurring Elliott Bay and the waterfront below into a runny watercolor of dribbling grays and blues.

Sam Rossi didn't see any of it. He chose not to. He chose to see what was important. That was his secret, how he had climbed to the top of the insurance jungle. Long after his employees had gone home, he remained at his desk and his desk faced the other direction, away from the window, away from the view, looking back into his office there on the 29th floor of the Yesler Tower. His office was important. His work was important and he was good at it.

Trim as a thirty-something, Sam was in his mid-forties, a smart, honest businessman with a good sense of timing and an instinct for deals. He went home at night to a nice house in a nice neighborhood. He made enough money to keep his family happy and give generously to his church. There was no way around it. Sam Rossi was a success. Because he knew what was important and how to pay attention to it.

"Hi, there."

His attention jumped to the unexpected visitor standing in the office doorway. It was long after hours. No one but the janitors should have been on the 29th floor.

Halfway to his feet, he realized who she was and his mouth fell open. It couldn't be. Her hair was different. She was different. This was no child. So how could this be his daughter? His Gina. His little girl who had gone away to college. Of course, she'd changed a lot after the first two years. He'd seen her at her mother's funeral. And now two more years had passed, but still — could it really be four years? Could she really have transformed herself into this breathtakingly beautiful young woman?

"It can't be."

"It's me, Dad."

For the first time that night, his computer screen and his tax deductions were forgotten. He stopped thinking about Rossi Insurance. All he could see was his daughter.

"Gina!"

They embraced.

"What an awesome office."

"Oh, that's right. You haven't seen this one."

"The last time I saw your office, it was smaller," she said. His marriage had come to an end when she was five. His ex-wife had moved to Tacoma, taking Gina with her. From then on she stayed with him six weeks every summer and every other weekend, until she left for college. "But I don't understand, Dad. Why do you sit with your back to the view? I mean, you've got this spectacular panorama and you sit facing the other direction. Why ignore it, when you've got so much of it?"

18

He smiled, his eyes bright with humor. "Too distracting," he answered. "A successful man keeps his mind on his work."

He thought she might be old enough to appreciate that. He could tell he was wrong. She was still a romantic, the kind who opt for looking at pretty views, and fail.

"So, what brings you on a visit to Seattle?"

"This is no visit," said Gina, laughing. "I live here now. After all, this is where my family lives."

He hugged her again. "What great news! Welcome to town. So, what don't I know? There's a secret in the air. Who's hired you? Where are you going to work?"

"I don't exactly have a job yet. I know that's an unimaginable state for someone like you, Dad, but don't worry, I have no intention of sponging off you. I've still got the money that Mom left me."

"I'm not worried about money," said Sam. "If I was, would I have insisted on sending you to Notre Dame? So, how's my young lawyer, anyway? At the head of your class?"

"Actually, I didn't end up majoring in law, or business, either. I decided I didn't want to spend my life making money off of other people's problems. Sorry to disappoint you."

"You don't disappoint me, Gina. You know I love you."

"I majored in landscape architecture."

"In what?"

"I'm going to be a landscape gardener."

"A what?"

"I'm starting my own business in the spring. It's called Green Thumb Enterprises. It offers custom landscaping at affordable prices — to people who don't make six-digit incomes."

"Green Thumb?" What more could he say? After four years of the best education money could buy, his daughter was becoming a glorified manual laborer.

Stunned, he listened in horror as Gina proceeded to tell him, in detail, about the humiliating mess she was making of her life. It got worse. She was living with some guy. That kid he met two years ago, at the funerals. He couldn't

19

believe his ears! Is that what he sent her to Notre Dame for? To learn how to shack up with some jerk, and forget all her values?

"I saved the most exciting news for last," she said. "I'm buying a house. Me, a homeowner! Can you believe it? And not just any house. I'm buying Nana's house."

Sam stared in disbelief. "You can't be serious. You're paying good money for that old pile of garbage?"

"Dad! How can you say that?"

"Because I know that house," he said. "It's a heap of troubles. That thing was built by a bunch of stubborn, stupid immigrants who didn't know what they were doing. Nothing built to code. Screwy plumbing. Dangerous wiring. You call that a good idea?"

"Dad, will you stop treating me like a child?" Her cheeks were flushed with anger.

"Will you stop acting like one?" her father countered. "What do you know about life? You've been handed all your money. You've never had a job. You're hardly twenty—"

"I'm almost twenty-three!"

"And so cocksure you've got it all figured out—" There was no stopping now. He told her exactly what he thought.

*

Sam Rossi remained sitting at his desk long after his daughter stormed out of the office. He was waiting for his heart to slow down. He became as motionless as the mahogany furniture all around him, deathly still except for his fingers. He couldn't make his fingers stop trembling. He put his hands on the desktop, and his fingers looked like they were tapping invisible keys.

Slowly he got his temper back under control. Now was not the time. He had to think clearly now. He did not owe his success in life to indulging his emotions. The secret was staying calm.

He switched off the lights in his office, turned his chair around, and looked out the window at the view.

Rain. Summer was over.

CHAPTER THREE

Halloween Intruder

1
Almost Nana's House

The icy sting of the wind sliced through the crack along the top of the car window.

Dead leaves leaped at the windshield, scratching at the glass, making sure Lou Rossi didn't fall asleep. It was Halloween afternoon. The kind of holiday that made him think about his grandchildren. How he wished they hadn't grown up so fast! He remembered helping Wally carve his first pumpkin, helping Rachel turn herself into a vampire with lots of red lipstick. He remembered saying the rosary by Gina's bedside, to help her get over the nightmares caused by scary Halloween movies.

And now Gina had bought his mother's house.

The deal had closed two weeks ago. Already all sign of habitation by Sokha Sok and family, not to mention Walter Woo and family before that, not to mention Remedios Del Donno and family before that, had been moved out, patched up and painted over, as though no one else had ever lived there after his mother, as though the house had never left the Rossi family.

It was almost Nana's house again.

Lou Rossi had seen to that. As a former real estate agent, he had been able to recommend to his granddaughter the best painters to re-do the entire interior, painting every room on all three floors. They had finished the job yesterday.

Lou sat in his car, parked across the street.

That was close enough, as far as he was concerned. He had not yet set foot inside. He would, of course, sooner or later. He was perfectly content for it to be later. He had gone inside often enough during those heartbreaking last years. He was in no rush. The house would wait for him.

Over eighty years old, the house stood stubbornly aloof and alone. It dominated the block, defying change, foremost among all the other aging, fading houses on Beacon Hill. Built in 1911, it squatted formidably in the middle of an oversized lot, in a yard of uneven lawns and intertangled garden-beds.

Lou had lived most of his childhood in that house. It had been built of wood when his father bought it. The hardworking, enterprising Niccolo Rossi had saved enough money to pour a new foundation and encase the original house in a veneer of handsome red brick, transforming the Rossi home into a fortress.

So many years had passed since then! That afternoon, parked in front of the old house, Lou could feel every year. His trim, well-clipped mustache was as jaunty and optimistic as it had first been in the Navy, but it had turned white. So had most of his remaining hair, and he still maintained a respectable amount. His cheeks had their share of wrinkles, but his skin was a healthy, weathered brown.

Just looking at that house made him feel older. He tried not to remember his mother's screams on that terrible last day.

He glanced up as a small black foreign car swerved in toward the curb. It left behind the person he'd been waiting for. Just the sight of her chased away the brief moment of gloom from his heart. Look at her! His granddaughter had grown into such a fine young woman.

Gina Rossi obviously hadn't recognized her grandfather's car yet. She wasn't looking in his direction. All she could see was the house. He knew, from her phone call, that she and her boyfriend were returning from some kind of social luncheon at the medical school. She was clearly dressed to impress, in a slim, blue sheath with a pearl necklace. A long, off-white overcoat blew open at her sides.

She stopped on the sidewalk before the front walkway. Lou could imagine how she felt. It was hers. She was taking an enormous first step in her life as an adult.

He got out of the car. She didn't hear his car door slam. She didn't notice him until he was standing beside her, poking with the toe of his shoe at the hole in the front lawn where someone had uprooted the "For Sale" sign.

"Not for sale any more," he said.

"Grandpa!" She hugged him. "Aaron just dropped me off. He'll be right back. He's gone to pick up something at Safeway. Well, what do you think? Isn't it incredible? Nana's house has become my house!"

He might have tried to answer her, but Lou couldn't look at the house yet without becoming tongue-tied. His granddaughter was too excited to notice.

"Isn't it like a dream come true? I can hardly believe it, Grandpa. This is going to be our new home."

Yes, yes. He nodded, with a smile. He understood. That house had been his home, too—

His parents had purchased the house back in 1917. As their only son, Lou had helped them after school selling fruits and vegetables on Beacon Avenue. Before long, Niccolo Rossi had saved up enough money from his long hours of hard work, endless sacrifices, and thrifty ways to purchase the entire building where he rented his fruit and vegetable stand.

Now all the other tenants paid their rent money to him. He and Orsola had conquered the New World. They had carved themselves a life in a strange, new city called Seattle. Unfortunately, they were not to share it together for long.

Lou was swept away from them by World War Two. He sailed off as an enlisted man in the Navy, into the sun-baked, treacherous waters of the South Pacific.

While Lou was at sea, one Saturday morning Niccolo Rossi reached up to weigh a dozen tomatoes on the scale, and unexpectedly collapsed into the vegetable display. He died five minutes later of heart failure, without warning, a handsome, healthy man of forty-three. From that day on,

Lou's grieving mother had lived in the house on Maynard Street alone.

Lou had married his pen-pal Gloria in San Francisco right after the war. He'd brought her back to Seattle, where they raised their two sons, Tony and Sam, in one of the Rossi apartments next door to his mother's house on Maynard Street.

Under Nana's constant, loving, intrusive eye.

Lou and Gloria's first son, Tony, had been Nana's unabashed favorite. Poor Tony! He had turned out to be a complete disappointment. In spite of scholarships and honors, he was unable to hold a job, unable to save money, and suspected of drug use. He had no interest in girls and wasn't likely to get married. No grandchildren to hope for there.

Their second son, however, had supplied what they most wanted. Sam's first marriage had resulted in Gina, his current marriage in Rachel and Wally. Three strong, healthy, polite grandchildren for Lou and Gloria to baby-sit and adore. Three great-grandchildren to be spoiled by Orsola Rossi, the tough old matriarch whom everyone in the family had come to call Nana.

"Come inside with me, Grandpa," said Gina, reaching for his hand. "Take a look."

"No, no," said Lou. "Not yet. I don't have to look inside, Gina. I know every inch of that house by heart. Believe me. Every inch."

The slinky black sportscar pulled up to the curb behind them with a confident purr.

"It's Aaron," she said, waving to the driver.

The car honked in reply, turned off its engine, and shuddered.

"I should go," said Lou uneasily. "I'll leave you two alone. I'm sure you have plenty of—"

"Oh, don't leave, Grandpa. At least say hello to him. You don't mind, do you? Please!"

"See, that didn't take long," said her boyfriend, climbing out of the car. "How's it going, Mr. Rossi?"

Lou smiled lamely. He raised his hand in a half-hearted wave. "Hi, there." He knew Gina well enough to see that it

24

was important to her. He had never been very good at saying no to his grandchildren. He would stay. He would talk.

But they would talk right there, on the sidewalk. Lou wasn't ready to go inside.

2
Red Rose, White Rose

"Your Grandpa didn't look very happy to see me."

They stood on the sidewalk together, watching her grandfather's car lurching back and forth, back and forth, nervously working its way out of the parking place.

"Nonsense." She waved after the departing car. "It had nothing to do with you. Grandpa's a little sensitive. For him, it's still his mother's house. He must have so many memories."

He put his arm around her. "Even more memories than you do?" She smiled up at him. His navy blue necktie was loose at the throat, his collar button undone. His expensive gray suit, like the flashy car, were graduation gifts from his parents.

She noticed the champagne bottle and plastic cups. The results of his trip to the store.

"Student supplies?"

"A little celebration is in order," said Aaron. "You and I have earned one."

"Hard to believe it's finally real," said Gina. She stood beside him on the walkway, facing the brick entranceway to the front porch. "There used to be a huge red rose bush on this side of the stairs and a matching white rose bush on that side. Which is exactly what I'm going to plant there."

"Sounds good to me," said Aaron, as he enfolded her from behind with his one free arm.

"Red on that side, white on that side. Or was it white on that side? Now, I'm not sure. I think the red was on that side, because I can remember red petals on the grass over here by—"

"You know, it doesn't have to be one-hundred-percent exactly the same."

"Yes, it does!" said Gina. "It does!" The words came out a little too fast, too emphatic.

And that look in her eye — there it was, again. That same look she'd had the day she told him she was buying the house.

"Every detail matters," said Gina. "Believe me, it all matters, and it's all going to be right. Red roses here, white roses there. I know exactly how it has to be."

3
Someone Inside

Together they started down the red-brick walkway toward the front door of their new home. Troubled clouds congested the sky into a premature darkness. The afternoon was drawing to a hurried, nervous end.

Halfway there, Aaron stopped abruptly, jerking her to an unexpected halt.

"What's wrong?"

He was squinting up at the house, shading his eyes with his hand. "Who was that?"

"Who?" Gina looked around her. "Where?"

"Somebody's in the house."

"How could they be?" said Gina. "Don't be a tease. It's my house now. I'm the one with the key."

"Obviously not the only key," said Aaron. She could see that he was serious. "Up there. Didn't you see that shadow in the window?"

"No."

"Don't look at me like that. Something moved. I could see a shadow distinctly crossing the light. Seriously, I swear. Probably one of the painters come back to pick up something they forgot." He cupped his hands around his mouth, and called, "Hello?"

No one answered.

"How could it be the painters?" said Gina. "Without notifying me? This house belongs to me now. Why would anyone need to be here, without my permission?"

"Misunderstanding," said Aaron, with a shrug. "I'm sure there's a perfectly good reason." He called toward the window again. "Hello, in there! Anybody home?"

"Well, they won't have a good enough reason for me," said Gina. "Nobody else has any business being in this house." She had her key out of her purse. She started up the stairs to the porch. "And I intend to make that very clear."

Aaron caught her arm.

"Let me take care of this."

"Am I looking particularly weak or helpless?"

"Things could get difficult."

"I may be just a woman but I can handle it. Make yourself useful. Hold the screen door open, would you?"

The lock clicked before the thrust of her key. The door swung open. Aaron tried to step in front of her, but she forced her way past him.

"After you," said Aaron.

Gina stepped across the threshold into the hushed emptiness of the house.

"Where's the light switch?" said Aaron, reaching out through the shadows along the living room wall.

But she had no interest in light. Her eyes were already adjusting. Before he could stop her, Gina had crossed the living room and was starting down the hall. Aaron was right behind her.

"Hey, slow down. Don't get all hot and bothered."

"I *am* hot and bothered," said Gina. "Whoever is in here doesn't belong here, period. This is my house, not theirs, and I've got the papers to prove it."

"Come on, Gina. It's Halloween. Kids go nuts at Halloween, do all kinds of crazy things. It's probably just some neighborhood hell-raisers who thought the house was empty."

"There's going to be some hell raised, all right," said Gina. "If I need a man to protect me, I'll holler."

27

"You know that's not at all what I mean," said Aaron. But he was talking to himself, left alone at the end of the hall as Gina started up the stairs. He didn't follow her. He knew better. "Fine, have it your way."

He stood nervously below. He heard her footsteps, heard her calling. He waited, every muscle tensed for the slightest sound, ready to bolt up the stairs.

No response.

He found himself standing alone. He paced down to the doorway of the master bedroom at the far end of the hall. Odd place for a master bedroom, on the main floor, but Gina had explained to him why. Nana had insisted. The three rooms where she would spend most of her time were all clustered together in a row — the room she shared with her husband, her son's room, and the kitchen. Why should she spend her day running up and down stairs? And she'd gotten her way. Nana must have been quite some woman.

As usual, Gina had insisted on following Nana.

He stepped into the empty bedroom. His footsteps rang hollowly across the wooden floor. He imagined where they would put the bed. He imagined them making love on it.

The room had three windows, a high one in the west wall that gave plenty of light and no view, and two bigger windows that opened north. One was in the perpetual shadow of a maple tree crowding that side of the house. The remaining window had a view of the backyard, and even a low wooden windowseat to accommodate the viewer.

He glanced out the window.

Because of the yard's steep slope, the house's main floor became, here at the back, an upper floor perched above the basement. The basement door opened beneath him, onto a stone path leading down to the vegetable garden.

Something about that little garden! He found himself staring at the scattered rows of leafy remains. And then he saw something else. Something that seemed to be moving through the garden, until he realized that it was not in the garden at all but reflected in the glass.

Something behind him.

"Gina?"

No one answered.

He turned around. No one. He turned back to the window. The reflection in the glass moved.

He spun around quickly.

"Very funny. Okay, I'm scared. You can come out now."

No response.

To his dismay, he found that he was getting jumpy. He stared intently into the glass. What was that? It was hard to see clearly, but something reflected behind him was shifting position in a corner of the hallway. Was it a person? Aaron wasn't sure. He could see it moving. He just couldn't see what it was.

Gina stepped through the bedroom doorway.

"False alarm," she said. "Nobody in the house but us." She surprised him by walking across the room and giving him a warm hug. He resisted at first. He wasn't so sure it was a false alarm. He kept peering out the door, down the hall, unconvinced. She convinced him. "Just us, and the smell of fresh paint."

"I'd say it's time to celebrate," said Aaron, attempting to shake off his weird mood. "Watch out."

The champagne cork ricocheted off the wall. The bottle frothed over. He caught the spill in the plastic cups. They interlocked arms and drank.

Their new life was officially beginning. The moving vans were scheduled to arrive early Saturday morning. One from Indiana, with the furnishings of both their college apartments. One from New Jersey, packed with a houseful of furniture from one of Aaron's wealthy aunts, recently deceased.

"We're on our way," said Gina.

"It's happening," said Aaron.

One drink led to another. After all, they really had something to celebrate.

"To a new life together on Maynard Street."

"I'll drink to that."

They drank.

"To the most wonderful person in my life."

"I'll drink to that."

They drained their plastic cups. Then they kissed. They kissed again.

"Happy Halloween."

"Too bad we don't have costumes."

"We don't need any costumes."

"Who can we be without costumes?"

"We can be Adam and Eve."

They couldn't stop giggling. They were like children. They started pulling off each other's clothes, unbuttoning, unzipping, in reckless excitement, there in the empty bedroom in the empty house. Gina's thin overcoat was hastily spread over the cold wooden floorboards.

"But there are no curtains on the windows—"

"So?"

"What if trick-or-treaters come?"

"We're wearing our costumes."

"Aaron!" She punched him in the shoulder.

He grinned. "Hey, if you stay down here on the floor where you're wanted, trick-or-treaters won't be a problem."

CHAPTER FOUR

Interrupted Thanksgiving

1
What Grandparents Are For

By November, Gina and Aaron were officially in residence, living out of cardboard boxes at 1716 South Maynard Street.

The chaos of floor lamps and dark oak chairs and boxes full of rattling, newspaper-wrapped dishes was arranging itself into a home. The kitchen had a toaster oven now, the bathroom had a second towel bar. The master bedroom was still mostly bed, but the bed was fine for a start. It was a good start.

There had been only silence from her father. No offer of help, no invitation to dinner. Not a word since their unfortunate exchange in his office. Her sister, Rachel, hadn't called, which meant Rachel hadn't found out yet that she was in town. She didn't expect to see much of her grandparents, either, considering how unhappy her Grandpa had become at the mere sight of his old home.

Her grandparents surprised her.

It hadn't been easy for Grandpa. His forehead had been lined with drops of sweat. He had insisted on coming up the back stairs. "We never used the front door when I was a kid," he said. Grandpa stopped in the middle of the kitchen, turning slowly around in circles, cracking his knuckles, a nervous wreck. "I feel like I just walked backward sixty years."

"I had to practically drag him here," said Grandma.

31

"I came on my own two feet," said Grandpa.

"So, where do we start, Gina? Put us to work. We're here to help."

And help they did. For the rest of the afternoon, and two days later, and the day after that, and the following weekend — dependable, hard-working allies.

Grandpa knew who to call about the hardwood floors, the new lock on the back door, the boiler inspection. Grandma helped her hang the drapes, organize her kitchen and her closets, and decide which lamp to put between which armchairs.

Her grandparents had been tireless that day, as usual, even after Gina had to leave. They were still working upstairs when she returned from her disappointing job interview at the Northwest Garden Center. She found them in one of the guest rooms. They'd put everything away, arranged the furniture, and were breaking down the empty boxes into a bouncy, floppy pile.

"How can I thank you? I don't believe how much you've done! Don't overdo it, now. I don't want you to be sore."

"I don't see your friend around," said Gloria candidly. "We could have used a little help with the heavy stuff. Why isn't he giving you a hand?"

"It's because he's in medical school, Grandma, that's why! He studies till he drops. He only has four hours left at the end of the day, and he has to use those for sleep."

"If you say so," said Grandma, unconvinced. She glanced at her watch. "Speaking of sleep, we should be getting home, Lou, before traffic gets too bad."

She helped them into their coats. They paused in front of the door, comparing their schedules for the next few days, planning when they would return.

Grandma kissed her on the cheek, and gave her hand an affectionate squeeze. "Now, we're going to see you on Thanksgiving, aren't we?"

Gina had sensed the issue hovering, unspoken, unresolved. "I don't think so, Grandma."

"And why not?" Grandma had clearly anticipated some resistance, and she was ready for it. "Now that you're back in Seattle, you're part of the family. Dinner is at two o'clock, and I want you both—"

"Not this time, Grandma. Things are a little tense with Dad."

"Makes no difference to me. You're still my granddaughter. Thanksgiving dinner is at my house and I'm inviting you. I want everyone there by—"

"You'll have a very nice dinner without me, Grandma," said Gina, kissing her on the cheek. "My Dad needs more time."

"What he needs is more love," snapped Gloria, "because you're his daughter and that's all there is to it. And as far as I'm concerned, Sam has no business—"

"Now, now," interrupted Grandpa. "You know perfectly well he's trying to be a good father."

"But he's making a big mistake!"

"You and I are going to stay out of this, Gloria." He turned to his granddaughter. "You and your boyfriend are welcome to join us for Thanksgiving dinner. But only come if you want to. There'll be no hurt feelings."

She hugged him again. "Thanks for understanding, Grandpa. We'll pass this time." She hesitated. "And if Rachel or Wally should happen to mention me?"

"If anybody asks," said Grandpa, "I've got nothing to say about Gina. Not one word." He looked at his wife meaningfully. "And neither do you."

2
The Trapped Animal

They had each other. It gave them strength. Nothing got in their way for long. Gina Rossi and Aaron Steiner were young and bright and determined, a winning team and they knew it, and the world seemed to know it, and for a while they almost seemed to be winning.

They celebrated Thanksgiving together that year in their new home, just the two of them.

She left him alone to study undisturbed all afternoon. Aaron had created a study out of the room between the master bedroom and the kitchen. That was where she found him, unshaven, in an old sweatshirt, hunched under his gooseneck lamp, textbook open on one side, computer screen glowing on the other. Gina touched him on the shoulder.

He shouted and leaped to his feet.

"Thanks," said Aaron, thoroughly shaken. "I needed that."

"Sorry," said Gina. "Getting jumpy, are we?" She kissed him. "I just came to tell the hard-working medical student that dinner is served."

"Say no more." He returned the kiss. "I'm starved."

"Your turkey awaits you."

She led him into the kitchen, to the little breakfast nook next to the pantry. The nook was scarcely big enough for a small table and two chairs, with a window looking down on the lawn and gardens below. The lights were off in the nook, and instead two slender white candles cast rippling shadows up the walls. Her best white tablecloth had transformed the kitchen table. Folded cloth napkins edged the two plates. Dressing and cranberries and a Jell-O salad flanked the turkey platter steaming between them.

"My first turkey cooked in Nana's oven," said Gina. "And for dessert, Grandma's recipe for pumpkin pie."

They kissed by candlelight.

"I'm the happiest medical student in the universe."

"And you'll soon be the fattest," said Gina. "I'm going to give you great big heaps of everything, just like Nana did. I'll be very insulted if you don't eat until you burst."

"I surrender," said Aaron. "Is stuffing your man to death an Italian tradition?"

"An ancient one. He dies with a smile on his face."

They sat at the little table facing each other, their hands clasped between the gravy pot and the bowl of mashed potatoes.

"I'm thankful for so much," said Gina impulsively.

"Me, too," said Aaron. "But I would be even more thankful with the pepper shaker near at hand."

Gina rose. "The chef is insulted but will comply."

She crossed the kitchen in a few quick strides and had just snatched the shaker off the shelf over the oven when something moved rapidly overhead. At first she thought something might have fallen. She stopped in her tracks, listening.

She heard it again. What in God's name could it be? A scramble of thuds passed directly above her, erratic, like footfalls.

Like something running.

Footfalls on the second floor? The thudding overhead seemed to rush to one side and then abruptly stop.

Aaron appeared in the entrance to the nook.

"Does the beautiful chef need help finding the pepper?"

She gestured him to keep his voice down. "Come here, Aaron. Listen." She pointed upward.

"What is—?"

"Just listen."

The look in her eyes alerted him to the depth of her concern. He froze.

Nothing. Just the sound of them breathing. He became restless. He reached out to grab the shaker out of her hand, and then they both heard it.

Footsteps in a shuffling rush across the floor overhead.

"What is that, Aaron?" She could see that he heard it, too. She wasn't crazy. Whatever was up there was real.

He looked up, squinting intently, as though trying to see through the ceiling. "Sounds like some kind of animal."

"Pretty big animal." said Gina, with a nervous laugh. "We're not talking mouse here."

A clattering surge of footsteps across the ceiling.

"It sounds as big as a dog."

"Well, I'm sure there's no dog upstairs," said Aaron.

"Then, what is it?"

"Could be a raccoon. It could be nothing but a squirrel, and the sound is being amplified somehow."

"A giant squirrel?" She stepped quickly and lightly over to the sink. Before he realized what she was doing, she had reached for her rack of glittering blades and grabbed the biggest chopping knife. "Well, whatever it is, I don't appreciate it interrupting my Thanksgiving dinner."

"Wait, Gina," he objected in alarm.

"No, thanks. I can handle a giant squirrel."

"Gina—"

She was already down the hall and around the corner, at the door opening onto the staircase that led up to the second floor. Aaron was right behind her.

Halfway up the narrow hall of stairs, they both froze and listened. When it came, it was so much louder. They both flinched when they heard it. Footsteps scuffling and frantic with haste, abruptly silent. Something was up there with them. Something as big as a dog, possibly injured, possibly frightened. Possibly dangerous.

They ascended several more steps, and then their legs refused to budge. They listened, braced to lunge back down the stairs. If the animal were hurt or scared, it could be fighting for its life.

Another clattering of footfalls.

"Look!" cried Gina, pointing. From where they stood near the top of the staircase, they could see partway down both the east hall and the west. Both were thick with shadows. Her finger stabbed toward the east hall. "There. What is that? See. It's moving—"

He didn't answer. He never said whether he saw it or not. He simply grabbed the chopping knife out of her hand and rushed toward the sound.

"Aaron, give me that!"

By the time Gina had hurried up the last two stairs and run halfway down the east hall after him, he was out of sight.

"Aaron?"

No answer. Nothing but a tense, unnatural stillness. Her footsteps echoed. "Answer me, Aaron. Where are you?"

Then suddenly, from behind her, the sound of running. She spun around in panic, not knowing which way to look, expecting imminent attack from any direction.

The footfalls abruptly stopped. But where? Where was the creature hiding?

Aaron stepped out of the far room.

"Nothing up here," he said. "Now, there's a mystery for you. Do you think it's just some weird sound made by the radiator pipes? Or maybe something's wrong with the boiler." He glanced at her, then did a quick double take on her fierce stance and wild-eyed pallor. "You okay?"

She forced herself to relax. "I'm okay."

They waited, rigid with nerves, expectant.

"You heard it and I heard it," said Gina. "It's up here. And we're going to find it."

Nothing. A dull, musty hush.

"I'm getting hungry," said Aaron.

"Well, I'm not leaving until I know what's up here."

They waited longer.

"Looks like our heavy-footed friend has something better to do. And so do we."

Frightened, confused, emotionally drained, Gina relented and followed Aaron downstairs. Closing the door to the staircase behind them, they returned to the breakfast nook. Flickering, half-melted candles illuminated a cold Thanksgiving dinner.

They didn't reheat anything. They chewed without tasting. They sat together in stunned silence.

"I don't believe what just happened."

"Pretty weird, wasn't it?"

"Tell me," said Gina. "Did you and I both just go crazy or what? Really, now. Was something running around up there? I mean, was that real up there, Aaron, whatever that was?"

"It sounded real to me."

"It sounded like something was hiding up there. Are we in danger, do you think? Or did we both eat something that's having a chemical effect on us? Are we hallucinating? Or psychotic? Or what?"

"I have a sinking feeling," said Aaron, "it's the *or what.*"

CHAPTER FIVE

Bad News

1
Getting Nowhere

The next day, and the next day, they waited anxiously for the mysterious footfalls to return.

Not a sound was heard upstairs. Not a squeaky board. Whatever had caused that alarming disturbance on Thanksgiving Day had apparently resolved itself.

Gina and Aaron gradually found themselves no longer tensing at the slightest sound. They resigned themselves to sharing and never understanding a mystery that no one else would ever believe. They turned their attention elsewhere.

They had other problems to worry about.

Aaron had expected medical school to be tough. It was overwhelming. He studied every night until his head hit the desk. He booked through every weekend. He sustained himself on triple shots of espresso.

"I've got to study longer."

"God didn't make days that long."

"I've got to sleep less."

"The human body can't function on less."

She tried to support him. She needed support herself. Her self-confidence was being shaken. Not only was the house taking up more time than she'd expected, but all of her promising job possibilities had, one by one, gone sour.

Until she started up Green Thumb in the spring, she had planned to get work in related fields, networking, getting to know the local industry. She'd wanted to brush up on Northwest specialties, learn evergreens, learn perennials. She narrowly missed a dream position at Rainy City Rockery, learning how to install paths, put in raised beds, construct arbors, vital hands-on grunt work. Tree Doctor considered her, but was really looking for a pruning specialist. For twenty-four hours she thought she had landed a job at Garden Management Services, until internal restructuring eliminated the position's existence.

Demoralized, Gina had abandoned hope of working in her field. She was ready now to settle for a steady paycheck. Clerk in a bookstore. Cashier in a supermarket. Receptionist for lawyers. Data entry at a hospital. All those smiling faces and firm handshakes and four-page applications should have led to something. All those nervous interview appointments and "You'll be hearing from us soon, Ms. Rossi," should have amounted to a job.

She was getting nowhere.

One by one, Gina Rossi was slipping through the cracks. She was under-qualified. She was over-qualified. She thanked everyone very much. She continued making copies of her resumé at the local copyshop. Money wasn't a problem yet, but what was left of the inheritance wouldn't last forever.

Then things suddenly got much worse.

2
Heat

It was impossible.

How could it be happening to her? How could she have forgotten to take her pill? Or was she just that terrible two-percent possibility? Desperately she hoped there was some kind of mistake.

She tested herself in the bathroom that morning. Her fears were confirmed. She managed to walk two steps, doubled over the bathtub, and threw up.

She refused to believe the test results. On a bitterly cold afternoon in the first week of December, she paid a visit to the doctor. She didn't tell Aaron.

She didn't turn on the lights when she got home. She didn't close the front door behind her. She got halfway across the living room in the dark and then sat down abruptly in her favorite chair, where she folded her arms across her chest and shuddered. Her shoulders hunched forward, shaking, as she quietly cried, waiting for Aaron to come home from the university.

By the time he got there, she was so lost in her own unhappiness that she didn't even notice.

"Gina?"

He stood on the edge of the living room, staring at her across the carpet as though she were on the other side of an uncrossable sea. "Gina?" he said to the figure in the shadows. "Do you realize that the front door was wide open? All the heat was going out."

"Heat?"

She stared at him, as though he were speaking a different language, with different values and concerns. She wasn't sure she could explain what had happened in that language. She didn't want to frighten him away. She didn't want Aaron to feel trapped. She didn't want to lose him. She was so worried about how to break the news to him she didn't notice that his eyes were as red and swollen as hers.

"Gina?"

She faltered for the right words, and then just blurted it out. "I'm pregnant."

Aaron forgot where he had intended to go. He sat down suddenly on the arm of the sofa. He had to sit there for a second, until the room stopped tilting. Then he gathered up what was left of his wits and control, and rose to his feet unsteadily. Slowly and with difficulty, he crossed the rug. He dropped to his knees by Gina's side and took her hand.

"I'm with you one hundred percent," he said. "Whatever we have to do."

His words might have caused her a wave of relief except that she finally saw his eyes.

"Aaron, what happened? What's wrong?"

He tried to say it without emotion but his voice cracked.

"My folks called this morning from New Jersey," he said. "It was a quizdown. A thousand questions. I got a little lost in the lies. So I gave up and stopped lying. They know now that we're living together. That their son is sleeping with a Gentile. My Dad was screaming. My Mom was sobbing. They just yanked all my funding. I've got to pay for medical school myself."

3
Breaking Point

Their bubble of happiness had collapsed. Money had suddenly become an issue.

An issue which Gina and Aaron carefully avoided talking about at dinner that night, keeping the conversation anchored in how the chicken had turned out, Grandma's recipes, winterization, kitchen plumbing. An issue which they put off discussing all evening and long into that sleepless night.

The issue of money.

And where it would come from. And how it was running out. How both were cut off now from their families. With no one to turn to but each other.

Which was the one place neither of them could turn.

Though they lay side-by-side in the darkness, both wide awake, far too troubled to sleep, their arms only inches apart, Gina and Aaron seemed to be separated by miles. Neither of them could break the silence.

The darkness thickened around the bed.

Aaron turned to look at Gina's face on the pillow beside him. A streetlamp halfway down the alley behind the house managed to pour enough light through the bedroom window to highlight Gina's wet cheek.

Without turning in his direction, she could tell he was looking at her.

"Aaron, I'm sorry," she whispered. She couldn't look at him. She stared straight up into the ceiling overhead. "I know I've been throwing you some real curves lately." Her wet eyes were making a mess of her face, as though they were melting in their sockets. "Buying the house. Without a word of warning. And now this. That girl is sure trouble, huh?"

"Gina, really! I'm just as much responsible--"

"You've got enough on your mind surviving medical school, without getting your landlady pregnant. So, Aaron, really, seriously — I don't mean to force you into saying or doing anything."

He didn't bother trying to explain away her fears. Instead, he kissed her wet cheek.

"As for your folks cutting you off, well — I can cover for you financially through winter quarter, at least. By then I'll have some kind of job until Green Thumb takes off in the spring. Which gets you through the first year."

He kissed her again. "One year of medical school is useless without a few more years, which I can't afford. Sounds like it's time to re-think a few goals."

"Aaron, no! Leave your goals alone. Give your parents a little time. They'll change their minds."

"Wrong," he said. "That's the difference between most Jewish parents and rich Jewish parents in New Jersey. Rich Jewish parents in New Jersey don't change their minds."

"We can make it without them," said Gina.

"If I could just find the right part-time job—"

"Job?" she echoed. "The human body requires sleep, even when it's a med student. How can you possibly work, and still get through school alive?"

"I can do whatever I have to do," he said, with all the idealistic stubbornness that made her love him.

She sighed. "I suppose that's the only thing you can do," said Gina grimly. "But how? How in God's name can I afford to have a child?"

Her words caught him off-guard.

"Have a child? I guess I misunderstood. You mean you're actually considering—?"

He could hardly think straight. The angry phone call from his parents had totally rattled him. Medical school had just been chopped out of his future. Because of his love for Gina, he would no longer be a doctor.

Should he calm down his parents by tactfully establishing a fake address in a rented room? Or should he abandon security altogether, and set out into an unpredictable future with a very unpredictable woman?

"I can't afford a baby," said Gina.

"I don't see how you can," said Aaron. "Where will the money come from?"

"I've got Green Thumb to consider," said Gina. "How can I start a business in the spring with a kid due in the fall?"

She started crying.

He squeezed her hand. "It's so hard. It's ours. I know you want it. I want it, too. But it's not the right time. Not financially, not emotionally. It just can't happen."

"Aaron," she said slowly, syllable by syllable, "I'm going to have the baby."

He stared.

She went on, not expecting him to understand. "It's not what I wanted. It's not what I expected. But I'm going through with it."

Aaron lay coldly beside her, as motionless as an effigy on a tomb.

"I've got to have it. Anything else wouldn't be me. I'm a gardener, aren't I? It's my job to cultivate life, my career to nurture life. Part of you and part of me are becoming something else. I've got to make sure that whatever is growing inside me gets a fair chance."

"While your father disowns you?"

"It's none of my father's business," she said. "He's not pregnant, I am."

He could feel her slipping away from him. He was losing her. "Are you sure you know what you're doing?"

She tried to answer him but nothing came out. She tried again. "Most of all, Aaron, what I'm trying to say is, I don't expect anything from you. This is my decision, entirely mine. Stay or go, it's up to you. There'll be no hard feelings. I don't expect a thing."

He tried to think of something to say. He opened his mouth, but the darkness of the bedroom poured into it, filling him with silence.

*

She didn't wake up until several hours later.

Whatever woke her clearly didn't disturb Aaron. He was snoring peacefully beside her.

There it was, again. She froze, listening. Was it somewhere in the room with them? She didn't think so. It seemed to be coming from down below, in the basement. She waited patiently for the sound to repeat itself.

There it was! What *was* that?

Time to put out the mousetraps.

CHAPTER SIX

Forbidden Sister

1
The Rossi Woman

Holidays attract accidents.

No doubt about it. Every holiday reinforced her theory, none more than Christmas. Dr. Helen Karr didn't care what anyone else thought of her grim principle of life, because her theory always proved true. There was no escaping it.

Holidays want accidents to happen.

Only seventeen days left until Christmas, and already the lobby of the Puget Sound Health Clinic was filling up before ten. Take away a couple nurses with the flu, and those left on their feet were doomed to an ugly, overcrowded day.

The Rossi woman was figuring in that day again. She was becoming a pain in the neck.

"Dr. Karr—" droned the impersonal switchboard voice.

She snatched up the nearest receiver. "Karr here."

"Ms. Rossi is waiting for you in Room Nine."

"You've got to be kidding me," sighed Dr. Karr. "I just talked to her an hour ago." An endless stream of nervous questions. Questions about nutrition. Questions about fetal development. Questions about emotional equilibrium.

"She wants to talk to you about gymnastics."

"Gymnastics?" She was certain she had misunderstood. What sane word sounded like gymnastics?

"Ms. Rossi would like your permission to compete in gymnastics."

Dr. Karr stopped in her tracks and turned toward Room Nine. Ms. Rossi was surely smart enough to realize that gymnastics was not a good idea for a pregnant woman. Though Dr. Karr usually behaved professionally, it had been a particularly long and unpleasant day. In three strides she crossed the length of the hall.

"Really, Ms. Rossi," she said, pushing open the door in exasperation. "Do you think gymnastics is appropriate for a woman in your condition? After all, there's a child to consider."

"What child?"

"You are Gina Rossi, aren't you?"

2
Finding Out

That was how Rachel Rossi found out. If she hadn't gone for her annual physical exam to compete on the high school gymnastics team, she might never have known.

Gina was back.

She was living in Seattle.

She was pregnant.

That was all she could think about as she drove north on the freeway toward home.

Christmas traffic was obscene. It was a gloomy, frigid December afternoon. Everyone was on the road, no one wanted to be there, and no one was concentrating on driving. Miserable faces grimaced behind every windshield.

Rachel grimaced right back at them.

She could read those unhappy faces, loud and clear. Each face was preoccupied with its own knot of worries, most of those worries revolving around Christmas and how close it was getting. About what they intended to buy, and where they were going to find it, and how much it would cost, and how they would manage to pay for it. The drivers on every side were pushy, neurotic, distracted, and rude.

And so was Rachel Rossi.

She was a stunning seventeen-year-old, with gypsy-black eyes and barely-manageable, shoulder-length hair. She loved driving. She was born to drive.

She could be just as belligerent, hard-nosed and aggressive as everyone else. She wasn't afraid to lean on the horn, or swerve in where angels feared to tread. She would rather have crashed and burned than have anyone even hint that she drove like a girl. She leaned down on the gas pedal, roared up and past the pokey Honda in front of her, then zipped in front of him and on over into the next lane. Honks of protest followed her little maneuver. Rachel didn't mind. This was Christmas traffic. You could drive like that at Christmas.

Except that Rachel wasn't thinking about Christmas at all. She was thinking about her pregnant sister, Gina. Who had finally finished college. Who had come back to Seattle. Who hadn't called her.

*

She parked in front of the handsome restored classic at the end of the cul-de-sac. Darting across the immaculate, manicured front lawn, she unlocked the front door, and went straight down the hall to the telephone. In a moment she was hunched over the kitchen drainboard, receiver tucked between shoulder and ear, furiously scribbling down the new address and phone number of Gina Rossi.

She punched the number into the telephone at once. She was almost dizzy with nervous excitement.

"Hello?" That treasured, familiar voice!

"Gina, it's me!"

"Rachel?"

"You'll never guess what happened. The doctor got us mixed up. She thought I was pregnant—"

Not until then did Rachel realize she wasn't alone in the house. She spun around. Her father was standing in the kitchen doorway. He was as shocked as she was. He was wearing a soaked T-shirt and sweats, the way he dressed when he took a break from his appointment-crowded day to work out at home on the Nordic Track. His mouth hung open in anguished disbelief. His cheeks slowly flushed red. Rachel stared at him in guilty terror.

"Hello? Hello?" said Gina's voice, tiny and far away. Her father snatched the receiver out of Rachel's hand.

"Gina," said her father.

"Dad?" She sounded like she couldn't believe her ears.

"Yes, this is your father." His voice quavered. "So, tell me," he said, his lips too close to the receiver, "is it true?"

Rachel strained to hear the voice on the other end of the line. "It's true," said Gina simply, bravely. "I'm pregnant."

He slumped backward against the wall with a groan. "How could you do something so stupid?"

"Dad, it wasn't on purpose—"

"Have you lost your common sense?"

"Look, I'm not going to defend myself. It was an accident. It happened. That's all there is to it."

"That's far from all there is to it. And just what do you plan to do now?"

"I'm going to have a baby, Dad."

"And no wedding-ring?"

"I can manage on my own."

"And what about the jerk who did it to you?"

"No one did it to me, Dad. We did it together. It was my fault as much as his."

"But you're the one who gets the shame. You're the unmarried mother. You're the disgrace."

"Disgrace? Do you feel like I'm a disgrace?"

"Am I supposed to be proud of you?"

"Would you rather I had an abortion? Is that what you want? Because that's an option, too." She was crying now. "It would be much simpler. I wasn't planning to have children. It's not a good time for us."

"Is it a good time to murder a child?" he whispered. Rachel had never heard so much anger in his voice.

"No one's murdering anyone," said Gina. "I'm going to have it. I'm sorry, Dad. I have to do what I think is right."

"Is that so?" he said. "Well, I have to do what I think is right, too. I do not want you parading around like that in front of your brother and sister. You are not welcome in this house."

He hung up. The click of disconnection rang loudly through the kitchen.

"As for you," he said, turning to Rachel. "You are forbidden to call her. You are forbidden to have anything to do with her. Don't test me, Rachel. I'm still your father."

3
A Good Catholic Queen

How Rachel hated him for that!

One lash of his hot temper and her sister was torn out of her life. She addressed her father only in monosyllables. They avoided each other. They ignored each other. The entire household was on pins-and-needles. Three tension-filled days passed, bristling with uneasy skirmishes.

Then Rachel entered the kitchen announcing, "You'll be interested to know that I've made another shocking discovery about the Catholic Church."

Her new thing was questioning Catholicism. Severely questioning its spiritual value, its role in history. It wasn't what her father wanted to hear. Sam Rossi had spent half his free evenings every week for the last ten years and far too much of his own money funding the Catholic school his kids attended. And now Rachel was attacking the very Catholicism which had so expensively nurtured her. As far as Sam Rossi was concerned, his daughter was rejecting more than a religion. She was rejecting her own father.

Every day Rachel discovered new historical atrocities committed by Catholics. She never failed to share these findings with her father, usually in the kitchen during the daily breakfast run-through, when all of their morning schedules briefly interconnected at the refrigerator, when her father's temper was often raw. Rachel never missed an opportunity of challenging the Church's degrading attitude toward women. She accused Catholicism of slaughters, purges, wars. Of atrocities against Jews and Muslims and heretics and Native Americans and gay people and just about half the planet.

She could have Sam Rossi fuming in minutes.

"I just can't believe it!" she exclaimed. "All these years I thought Queen Isabella was such a great person. You know, uniting all of Spain in Catholicism. Believing in Christopher Columbus. Financing the discovery of the New World."

"You thought right," said her father.

"Wrong," said Rachel. "Now I'm finding out the truth."

She knew he would ask. "And what is the truth?"

"The truth," said Rachel, "is that first she drove all the Muslims out of Spain using Jewish money. Then she drove all the Jews out of Spain and made them leave their money behind. Do you know how many hundreds of thousands of Spanish Jews were driven out of their homeland?"

"You're exaggerating again," said her father tensely.

"Forced out to sea in overcrowded ships. Delivered to the tortures of the Inquisition. Dumped on islands where they were eaten by savage animals."

"Rachel, you're going to be late to school," said her mother nervously. But Rachel wasn't quite finished.

"And get this — Queen Isabella had choirboys appointed to sing near her throne, so she wouldn't be disturbed by the screams of the Jews and heretics being tortured."

"Where do you get this kind of crap?"

"It isn't crap!"

It was another battle royale.

Rachel stormed out of the house. By the end of school, she was ready to defy the unfair ban on her sister. When the last bell rang and the other girls on the gymnastics team headed toward the locker room to change clothes, Rachel darted out the back door of the gym, car keys in hand. She was soon behind the wheel and heading for the nearest entrance ramp to the freeway.

It was time to defy her father's ridiculous ruling. What right did he have to separate her from her sister? Besides, how would he ever know?

4
The Back Porch

She was on her way to see Gina!

Rachel reached forward and changed the radio station. Anything but Christmas carols. She settled for Butterfly Jam playing "Ain't No Use." Her running shoe tapped out an accompaniment to the tune.

> *No one tells me what to sing*
> *Or how I gotta dance*
> *I've got my life to live*
> *Give me a chance*

She banked around the entrance ramp to Interstate-5. Too bad about skipping practice, but she wasn't worried. They wouldn't kick her off the team. She was their best all-event competitor and the coach knew it. Athletic competition had always come easily to Rachel, especially since it was such a surefire way of impressing her father. She was naturally athletic, naturally coordinated, and smart as a whip. She drove the boys wild but avoided them. Boys always disappointed her.

As did her parents. Her father, in particular.

The very thought of him now made her angry again. She noticed she was gripping the steering wheel. The speedometer was rising. How stubborn he could be. How narrow. How blind. How wrong.

And how infuriating!

Ever since Rachel had gotten her driver's license last year, she had become independent, defiant, volatile, and in the opinion of her father, impossible. She had begun openly challenging her father's ideas, and squealing off to a friend's house whenever things got too hot.

Like now. Except this time she wasn't going to Lucy's.

The yellow fortress of Rainier Brewery crouched by the side of the freeway as Rachel swerved over toward the Columbian Way exit.

The exit to her forbidden sister's house.

A few moments later, she pulled up in front of 1716 South Maynard Street. The sight of the familiar old house made her hit the brakes. She bounced one wheel up on the curb. The tires scraped. She'd had no idea until then. Nana's house.

She slammed the car door behind her. Halfway across the parking strip, she came to a faltering stop and just stared. She couldn't believe it! She still had fuzzy memories of that house, from when she was very young.

With a surge of excitement, she set out across the lawn, heading around to the back door on the side of the house. She was eager to see her sister again. Gina had been the idol of Rachel's childhood, the pretty older sibling whose body had begun changing in such wonderful ways while Rachel was still wearing braces. Her childhood devotion to Gina had been legendary in the family.

She hadn't phoned ahead. She wanted to surprise her.

She trotted up the flight of eight stairs into the little back porch. It was hardly bigger than a telephone booth. The moment she stepped inside it, Rachel remembered the claustrophobic feeling it had always given her during Nana's last years. Every available inch of that porch had once been crowded with plants. Two levels of shelving had leaned up against the windows, where limp and withering leaves had jostled and poked each other for room to bake in the sun.

They were not just random plants, Rachel had discovered. All of them had one thing in common. They were ailing. Some were dying, some not far from it. The sick and terminal of Nana's plant kingdom had been sent to the back porch for a last dose of life-sustaining sunlight.

Little Rachel, in her earliest memories, had hated and feared that porch.

It was currently benign and unimpressive. No longer filled with dying plants, it contained only a few empty boxes waiting to be recycled out back.

She rapped on the door. She waited and rapped again. Too eager to wait, she tried the knob. It turned. Not locked? Gina must be nearby.

Rachel swung the door open, and leaned into the empty, old-fashioned kitchen. "Hello!" she called.

Her voice echoed through the emptiness of Nana's house while she waited for Gina to appear. In a moment, her sister would find her standing there, unexpected, unannounced, inside the little back porch. In a moment, she would be throwing her arms around Gina's neck.

"Hello—" she called again, louder this time, into the familiar old kitchen.

She remembered that kitchen only too well. That was where an ancient old woman named Nana had once, long ago in Rachel's earliest childhood, sat reading the newspaper in her wooden chair by the warmth of the oven door. An old woman who always had strange, stinky vegetables cooking on her stove, who always clutched Rachel and kissed her and blessed her and terrified her.

"Hello—"

No one answered.

5
In the Cantina

Rachel was ready to give up and leave in frustration, when one last call got a faint response.

"Down here," came a voice from the open door on the other side of the kitchen. There, at the beginning of the hall, a lighted doorway opened onto a staircase, which descended steeply into the basement.

Rachel pattered down the wooden stairs. The vast, empty basement was deserted. No sign of her sister. Had she been hearing things?

"Hello—?"

"In the cantina."

"In the *where?*"

"Over here."

Beyond the old washtub and clotheswires, up three wooden stairs, was a dwarf-size doorway. Inside, a single

60-watt bulb dangled from one of the beams of the low ceiling. Its stark light glimmered on rows of wooden shelves inside the cement walls of a small, white-washed underground wine cellar.

"Sis!"

Gina was crouched at the far end, in blue jeans and a shirt with rolled-up sleeves, intently busy under one of the shelves.

"Rachel!" she cried, smiling with delight. "What a great surprise!" She rose at once, not quite to her full height beneath the low ceiling. "Watch your head," she advised her sister, a moment before she swept her into her arms.

A long, warm hug.

"It's so great to see you!" said Gina.

"You look fantastic," said Rachel admiringly. "What are you doing down here?"

"Just putting out some mousetraps," said her sister, grinning at her. "We've got a few more housemates than we bargained for."

"Great," said Rachel, glancing around her uneasily.

"They've been terrible the last few nights. What a racket! Enough to drive peace-loving people to murder." She carefully set out another baited trap. "It took you long enough to get back to me."

"You're off limits now."

"I suspected that might be the problem," said Gina. "So, are you going to get in trouble for coming over?"

"Only if he finds out," said Rachel.

"Be careful, okay? I don't want to make things hard for you in the family."

"Hey, I'm a big girl now," said Rachel. "I can take it."

"So, what do you think?" said Gina, gesturing with her arms to include the whole house above them.

"Nana's house," said Rachel. "I didn't realize. I'm still in shock."

"It was for sale, so why not? Do you remember this crazy little room? How about these?" She pointed toward two big wooden barrels taking up one end of the cantina. "They're still here. No more wine in them, though."

Rachel's face lit up. "I do remember. Grandpa used to make wine down here. I remember the grapes going through the wringers, and getting all crushed and smashed into this gross, juicy mess, and feeling sorry for the grapes—"

"You would," said Gina.

"Don't give me trouble."

"Grape-lover."

They both laughed. Rachel wandered down the length of the cantina, ducking her head beneath the low beams of the ceiling.

"I remember this place. This is where Nana always came to get the antipasto and the pies."

The two sisters looked each other in the eye at the same time. Then they cried out simultaneously, like a chant from the past, the name of Nana's mouthwatering specialty. "Wild blackberry pie with ice cream!"

They enjoyed laughing together. Just like old times. How Rachel had treasured their two weekends a month together! The six-week summers they used to share, before Gina went off to college, had invariably ended in tears.

"There used to be all those glass jars full of olives and chopped up vegetables on the shelves, remember?"

"Do I remember?" Rachel scrunched up her nose to show how much she remembered. "And floating pickled things."

The sisters started getting giggly.

"I loved this house," said Rachel. "But it was always sort of scary, too, don't you think? Just like Nana was sometimes a little scary."

"She scared you?"

Rachel was no longer giggling. "When she stopped combing her hair, and started running around in her nightgown, and hiding in those spooky rooms upstairs."

"She only got that way at the end—" But Gina remembered their last visit to Nana's house only too well.

"Remember, when we went to see her," said Rachel, "and she didn't know who we were anymore. And she started screaming, and Dad made us wait for him in the car."

"That was just at the very end."

6
The Impossible Baby

"You remember Aaron. You met him a couple years ago, when Mom died."

"Sure, I remember him. A real hunk. You two really hit it off, huh?"

"I guess you could say that."

Not until almost an hour later did they get around to mentioning what was on both of their minds.

"So, how are you feeling?" That was as close as Rachel could get to the topic of pregnancy. They were sitting side by side on the cantina stairs.

"Fine," said Gina.

"It must be incredible."

"It's pretty incredible, all right."

"You and Aaron must be so excited."

"Yes, well, Aaron and I are certainly very—"

Rachel thought her sister was searching for the right word. Then she realized she was crying. "Gina, what is it?"

Gina wiped at her eyes with the back of her hand, tried to smile, tried to lie to her sister. She couldn't. "I'll tell you what it is. It's a nightmare."

"What are you talking about?" said Rachel. Her sister was scaring her. "Is something wrong with the baby?"

"Something's very wrong with the baby." She stared across the basement, as though the answer lay somewhere on the other side, beyond the basement door. "The baby is the worst thing that could possibly happen. It's going to destroy what Aaron and I have. He's doing his best to be a good sport about it, but he's feeling trapped, I know he is, I can see it in his eyes. And I'm feeling trapped, too, trapped in my own body."

"Don't you want the baby?"

"No, I don't want the baby." The words came out with unexpected hostility. "The baby is impossible. The baby is all wrong. It can't happen. It — it isn't going to happen."

Rachel felt uncomfortable. She didn't want to know any more, but she couldn't stop asking. "What do you mean?"

Gina hadn't intended to tell her. Not until she started pouring out her feelings to her sister did she realize how much she needed to talk to someone. "I've made a decision. The only sane decision I could possibly make. I'm going to have it — taken care of. I have an appointment at the doctor's tomorrow morning."

For a tense moment, the two sisters sat on the cantina stairs in silence, not looking at each other.

Rachel spoke first. She could hardly assimilate what she had just heard. "Is that what Aaron wants you to do?"

Gina hesitated. "Aaron doesn't know."

"Oh, my God."

"I don't have any choice." The words rushed out of Gina. "I have to do something. I just want this nightmare to end. It will be such a relief to get it over with."

"But aren't you scared?" The very thought of it made Rachel feel faint. Not to mention trespassing onto such frightening moral ground.

"Of course, I'm scared," said Gina. "But it's the only way out of this mess. The only way." The sight of so much fear in her younger sister's eyes made Gina reach out and take Rachel's hand. "Don't worry. Everything will be fine."

"I know it will be," said Rachel. She tried her hardest to act like an adult. "It will be fine."

"Even though Dad will never forgive me."

"Dad!" The mere mention of her father was all Rachel needed. Now she was on familiar ground again. "Dad doesn't live in the nineties," she said. "He's off in his own little Catholic dreamworld."

"If Dad found out, he'd go through the ceiling."

"He'd have cardiac arrest. Well, if he gets uptight, so what?" She regarded her sister's tear-streaked cheeks. "Sis, do you want me to go with you?"

"Thanks." Gina was touched, but she had already made up her mind. "No, I can handle it. By tomorrow this will all be over. We'll pretend like it never happened."

7
Mousetrap

Someone had to change the subject, and so Rachel did. "What are you going to do for Christmas?"

"Absolutely nothing," said Gina.

"You're not coming home?"

"You've got to be kidding. How can I come home, if Dad refuses to have me in the house? As far as I'm concerned, I've been disinvited. It's no big deal. Christmas doesn't mean that much to me. Besides, I have Aaron now. He and I will celebrate somehow, very low-key. He isn't Christian, after all. But a big family Christmas? It isn't going to happen. And that's fine with me."

"I guess. If that's how you feel." Rachel shrugged, not really showing her own feelings on the matter. She glanced at her watch. "Yike!" she said, rising abruptly to her feet. "I better get back before they send out the police."

Gina rose, too. "Thanks for coming, sis."

"I miss you so much." The two sisters hugged. "Good luck tomorrow. Just forget about Dad. You know what's best. Get it over with. Do what you have to do—"

A sudden, loud crack! Something leaped at them out of the shadows. They both screamed. Wood clattered at their feet. Another loud wham-smack! This time from the other side of the cantina. They tried to turn around, this way, that way, not sure where it was coming from next. Something hit one of the shelves. Another sharp, snapping bang. Something flipped over on the floor, shuddering.

"What is it?" cried Rachel. "What's happening?"

A hush in the cantina.

The two sisters gripped each other. Slowly Gina drew away and looked down at the floor.

There, by the toe of Rachel's running shoe, metal tongue dangling, lay an overturned mousetrap. Another mousetrap lay in the corner. Another had fallen off the shelf. They had been snapping and popping on all sides.

"Mousetraps?"

"I just set them."

"But why did they all go off?"

"Must have been a real fast mouse," said Gina, stunned. "Either that, or I don't know how to set mousetraps."

"All at the same time," mumbled Rachel. "Weird."

"Incompetent is more the word for it," said Gina. "Don't you dare tell Aaron. I'd never hear the end of it."

"Your secret is safe with me," said Rachel. She breathed a sigh of relief. "I better get out of here. I'll leave you to your mousetraps." She kissed Gina on the cheek. "I can show myself out." She hesitated. "Good luck tomorrow."

"Thanks, sis."

Halfway up the stairs, she called back down, "Do you really want me to leave your back door unlocked?"

"Lock it," said Gina.

Rachel scampered up the stairs. As she passed through the kitchen where Nana had sat by the oven, she felt a wave of guilty relief that her great-grandmother was dead. Nana had genuinely frightened her. Rachel hated the thought of growing old and ugly and wrinkled, forgetting everything, going crazy.

She crossed the kitchen, flipped the lock, then carefully pulled the kitchen door shut behind her until she heard it click securely.

Not until it was locked did she turn around to face the door of the back porch. With the first twist of the knob, she realized that something was wrong. The porch door seemed to be jammed. She jiggled it, rattled it. Oh well, she would have to get Gina to let her out. She tried to return to the kitchen. The kitchen door was locked tight.

She twisted and turned the knob of the porch door, glaring out the back window at the world on the other side, just out of reach. She rattled the porch door fiercely. It refused to tug free. In exasperation, she began hammering with her fist on the kitchen door.

"Gina!" she called.

She had an uncomfortable feeling that Gina, being down in the cantina, wouldn't hear a thing. Of all places to get stuck! She wondered how long it would be before her sister came upstairs. How many mousetraps did she have to re-set?

She tried to wait patiently. One long, slow minute dragged into another. And then she began to smell an unpleasant odor. What was that sweet and sickening smell? It was vaguely familiar — and then she knew what it was. She associated that smell with this very back porch.

It was the slimy rot of dying plants.

But how could that be? There were no plants in the back porch now. Where could that nauseating odor be coming from?

"Gina!" she shouted. She banged with her fists. She was much too tough to admit to herself that she was getting scared, but she was starting to lose her grip. She could feel herself edging toward panic.

The stink of rotting plants was getting worse. And something else. It was getting so cold on the back porch. Was there a crack somewhere? She could feel an icy draft on her legs. Something about that chill—

"Gina!" she screamed. Her voice rang too loudly in the tight, little porch, but there was no sign that she had been heard inside. She pounded with both fists. She clutched the doorknob, tugging on it. She became so frightened, she started to cry, sobbing like a child. In the middle of a sob, the door latch came unstuck.

The porch door swung gently, easily open.

Rachel flung herself out of the back porch, down the back stairs, and across the lawn. She ran all the way to her car. She never told anyone what happened, not even her sister.

CHAPTER SEVEN

Forgotten Staircase

1
Hot Words

Gina loved her little sister dearly, but after an hour of Rachel's intense company, she was glad to be alone. She needed quiet. She needed to gather her thoughts.

What could have caused all the mousetraps to go off? She picked them up one by one, examining them by the light of the dangling bulb, mystified. None of the little bits of bacon had been touched. Could there be a defect in the spring? Too many little mysteries were going unsolved.

But the house was worth it. The house had become her passion. She loved working on it, restoring the Nana's house of her memory, making her home in a place that had been the very heart of the Rossi family. The house first — and then, in the spring, the gardens. Each destined for unique arrangements, giddy waves of color. Not to mention that vegetable garden in back. Something about it tugged at her heart, even in the middle of December. Something compelled her to thrust a shovel down into the soil.

But she had enough to do indoors.

The afternoon did not proceed smoothly. A quick lunch became not so quick when she splattered milk all over the kitchen floor. Halfway down the back stairs, in an attempt to empty the trash, the garbage bag broke in her arms, spilling something unspeakable down the front of her.

While washing it off in Nana's old-fashioned bathtub, the telephone rang. Clutching her towel around her, dribbling water down the hall, she managed to reach it in time. She wished she hadn't. It was her stepmother, Barbara Rossi.

"Hi, Gina," she said. She sounded cheerful and upbeat. One never knew with Barbara. "Welcome back to Seattle. How's everything going?"

And so forth. Polite nothings. She followed Barbara's lead, making small talk, waiting until she worked her way around to the real nitty-gritty.

"I don't suppose Rachel is there, by any chance?"

"Rachel?" So that was it. "Why would she be here?"

"No reason in particular. Just a hunch."

Gina had never been completely at ease with her father's second wife. She loved Barbara, of course, and Barbara loved her, of course. But something had always been missing. Neither Gina nor Barbara quite trusted each other.

"Why? Has anything happened to Rachel?" She was admittedly playing dumb, but she wanted to get Barbara talking. It never hurt to hear the other side.

"No, no," said Barbara evasively. "Nothing to worry about, I'm sure. One of her friends just called. I guess Rachel didn't show up for gymnastics. You know your sister. She just takes off with the car. Doesn't tell anyone where she's going."

"Why would she do that?" persisted Gina. "Has Dad been getting on her case?"

Barbara had no intention of talking about that particular issue with her stepdaughter "I understand you had a few words with your father yourself."

"You could say that," said Gina. "You could say he had a few words back. I expect he told you the news."

"Yes, he told me." That was all. Barbara avoided uncomfortable topics. "He doesn't always mean what he says, Gina."

"I don't care what he means or doesn't mean. He is not going to tell me how to live my life."

"Your father worries about you."

"Is that so?" said Gina. "I doubt if he's worrying too much. If he was, he'd be making this phone call himself."

"Now, you know what he's like," said Barbara. "His religion is such a big part of him. He's very concerned about you. He's just stubborn, that's all. He's a Rossi."

"I'm a Rossi, too, and just as stubborn, and I intend to make Nana's house into my house, and do what I have to do, and I don't care what my father thinks, and you can just tell him — tell him Gina says Merry Christmas."

Click.

2
The Wrong-Way Door

Fuming with hostility and hurt feelings, Gina finished drying her hair and got dressed. Then she gathered up her cleansers and sponges, dustrags and mops, and stomped up the staircase.

She had been working upstairs that week and had reached the far bedroom at the end of the east hall. It was one of her favorites. It was remote enough that it was out of hearing of both doorbell and phone, and the closets were huge.

All of the east rooms had been closed off when Gina was a child. Of course, being forbidden, they had been recklessly explored behind Nana's back by her daring great-grandchildren, but the rooms had been a boring disappointment. They were packed wall-to-wall with stored furniture. Not much incentive to risk a scolding. The rooms of the west hall, on the other hand, had bounceable beds and sliding rugs and plenty of playing area. The east hall had been ignored.

Until now. Now its three rooms were like new additions which had no place in her memory, bonus rooms besides all the familiar rooms of her past.

She had washed the windows of the far eastern room, aired it out, swept it out, dusted it out. She had arranged a spare bed, a desk, a couple mismatched chairs, an old bureau, a throw-rug. She was just about to start polishing an old mahogany end table when a lingering glance of admiration into the room's walk-in closet brought to her attention a small door.

It was at the closet's far end, too short to be a broom closet, too large to be a laundry chute. She vaguely remembered noticing it before. She had always intended to find out its purpose, and always forgotten about it.

"Incredible," she mumbled. "All the little nooks and crannies." The old house never ceased to amaze her. She crouched down in front of it, turned the knob, clicked the latch, and pulled. The door wouldn't budge. Then she pushed and the door swung inward.

It was so odd it made her laugh. She never knew which way doors would open in that house! She poked her head inside.

A tiny window up at the top, gray with grime and cobwebs, provided just enough light to see. A steep, narrow staircase, scarcely wide enough for her shoulders, seemed to lead up to some kind of attic. More room! She had never seen so much storage space. What a weird little staircase. It couldn't possibly be any tighter.

She switched on the closet light behind her, but the overhead bulb had no impact on the stairway. She considered going downstairs for a flashlight. Why bother? The gray light filtering through the little window illuminated the edges of the stairs. Her eyes would soon adjust to the darkness.

She ducked through the door, reaching out toward the far wall. Her hand disturbed a thick veil of cobwebs, which clung to her fingers and became stuck in a long streamer across her face, in her hair. She angrily beat it away.

She sniffed at the stale air and took another step. A brittle snapping crunch underfoot. She drew back with a shudder. What had she stepped on? Dried mouse bones? Bird bones? Too dark to see. She didn't want to know, anyway. She just wanted to see where the staircase led, and then do some serious cleaning.

Step by step, she made her way up the tight passageway. Not an inch to spare. The door would have to be completely unhinged and removed to store anything of size up-stairs in the attic. Or wherever the little staircase led.

Up another stair and another, brushing her shoulders on either side. But to where? She kept waiting to see around the corner, but the corner never came. The stairs just seemed to stop at the window. The secret of the staircase was that it led nowhere.

"How very strange," she said. "Oh, well. Maybe that's just how old houses are. Lots of little crazy stuff."

She ran her fingertips over the window glass and immediately wished she hadn't. Accumulated grime slithered off in a gob. The windowsill was a dusty graveyard for the shriveled corpses of spiders and flies.

Turning around at the top of the narrow stairway, she started back down. "Maybe meaningless staircases were something that pioneer Italians liked in their houses," she muttered. "Maybe it was considered very stylish to have stairs in your closet that led nowhere."

She was careful enough to place her feet securely on each stair. Step by step, she descended. Then she paused.

She heard another step behind her.

Gina spun around, startled, banging her elbow into the wall. She took a sudden step backward toward a stair that wasn't there.

She landed sitting down, with a hard smack. The back of her head clattered against the door, slamming it shut. The fall knocked the breath out of her, scared her. What had she just heard? Now she had only one goal. To get out of there.

She twisted her arm up toward the knob. She could reach it, but couldn't turn it. She tried to shift position, to get up on her feet. An icy chill shuddered down her spine. Had she torn a muscle? Pinched a nerve? She tried not to panic.

"Just catch your breath," she coached herself, "count to ten, and use your brains."

She never got a chance to try. She was still in the breath-catching phase when she heard it.

Thong—

67

A hollow thud on wood.

Thong—

Another smack.

Thong—

Something with a rubbery impact.

Then silence. Followed by another sound, so soft at first that she wasn't sure she heard anything at all. Slowly, slowly louder, until there could be no doubt what it was.

Somewhere up at the top of those stairs, a child was crying. A very unhappy little kid was somewhere right there in the house with her.

Gingerly, painfully, Gina righted herself and scrambled up onto her knees, straining her neck to see anything at the top of the staircase.

The temperature seemed to get abruptly cooler. What could cause such an icy draft? Could a window be broken somewhere upstairs?

Then she sensed another presence.

She squinted into the dimness. A movement at the top of the stairway. But she had just been there. The stairs went nowhere. Something seemed to shift position slightly in the corner of her eye. What was that?

Gina felt her whole body go numb with fear.

It didn't look solid. She blinked. It was a shadow, just a shadow. She blinked again. No, it wasn't.

That was someone.

Not a child. Too big to be a child. Someone who began to make a sound. Such a sad sound!

"Who's up there?" she managed, in a hoarse whisper.

No answer.

Then she saw the eyes. Terrible, unhappy eyes. The shape seemed to lunge at her. An icy chill passed through her. She heard someone sobbing, as though all reason for living had been lost. Repeating a word over and over that Gina couldn't quite understand, a foreign word she'd never heard before.

It sounded like "—Ito! —ito!" It was the saddest word Gina had ever heard in her life.

3
Possessed

That was how Aaron found her when he got home from his classes, wedged into the bottom of the narrow staircase in the far closet upstairs. He ran bounding up the stairs, lunging from room to room, tracking her cries.

"Gina, it's me!" he shouted. "Where are you?"

When he finally got her to move enough to push open the door, she collapsed out of the staircase into his arms.

"Gina! Are you hurt?"

"I'm all right," she said, clutching his arm. "I'm not hurt. I'm scared. I'm just scared out of my wits."

"Scared of what?" he said.

"I don't know what. I think I heard a child crying."

"A child? Where?"

"Here. Right here in this house. Some unhappy little kid. And then — then I saw her."

"Saw who?" said Aaron. "Was someone else here with you? You're not making sense."

"She was so sad, she was wailing, this awful sound—"

"I don't understand. Where was this?"

"Right in there. At the top of those stairs. But it's all okay now, because I know who it was. It's obvious."

"What's obvious? Gina, I think you may be more hurt than you realize."

"It just makes sense. I mean, I should have expected it, Aaron. It was Nana."

"Your great-grandmother?"

"I don't understand the crying yet. Or the thudding sound. But that voice. It was Nana's voice."

"Gina, you know perfectly well that your Nana—"

"It was her," said Gina, with a weird confidence. "And she was so unhappy, shouting something. And it got so cold. Like she went right through me. But the whole thing, well — it knocked some sense into me."

"Sense?" echoed Aaron, laughing in amazement. "I'd say that's an item you're a little short on at the moment."

"Real sense," she qualified, as though that said it all. "It was like she touched me, Aaron. She woke me up, and now I can make a beginning. Now I know what to do, where to start."

"For someone who's just had some sense knocked into her, you're not making a bit of it."

She looked into his eyes, seemed to consider his words, and then weakly nodded. "I think you're right," she said. "It's too soon to make sense."

"Much too soon." He kissed her forehead. "I think you must have hit your head, and had some kind of scary dream."

"I definitely hit my head," said Gina, gently fingering the back of her skull. "But it didn't seem like, well — I'm not sure, except — Aaron, I've decided something. I've got to cancel my doctor's appointment tomorrow."

"Doctor's appointment? What doctor's appointment?" He was immediately alarmed. "Gina, is something wrong? What is it I don't know?"

"I just thought — well, I decided — I was afraid the baby would drive you away, and — well, I don't want to lose you, Aaron. So I decided not to have it."

"Gina, Gina, I already told you—"

"And I'm not going to have it, it's just that—" She faltered, began again. "I want to wait until after Christmas, that's all."

"Gina, I'm not asking you to do anything—"

"I'll take care of it right after Christmas. Something has to be done, and I'll do it. But tomorrow's too soon. I can't do it tomorrow." She took a deep breath. "I need to rest. I'm exhausted. I shouldn't be trying to talk about it."

Which sounded calm and reasonable, and should have comforted him, except that he happened to glance in her eyes and saw the look again. That disturbing, determined, glazed look. That look she sometimes got when she talked about Nana's house.

"No need to discuss it now," said Aaron. "Come on, put your arm around my neck. Let me help you downstairs. One thing at a time. Call the doctor and cancel your appointment."

She obediently wrapped one arm around his neck, and then hesitated mid-step. She almost told him what else she had decided.

She opened her mouth and then shut it.

Not yet. Tomorrow would be soon enough. "Yes, one thing at a time." She would tell him about her plans tomorrow.

4
Disaster in the Making

She spent all night in his arms, and didn't give him one hint of the change that had taken place inside her.

Not until the next morning, in their bathrobes, snuggled together on the same side of the tiny breakfast nook, did Gina mention what she was going to do.

"You've got to be kidding," said Aaron.

"Not kidding."

"But *why* would you want to do that?"

He stared at her, waiting for the first hint of a smile, hoping for a slow punchline.

None came.

"I've made up my mind," said Gina. "So don't try to talk me out of it. I've never been so sure of anything in my life. This Christmas the Rossis are going to have a big, old-fashioned family dinner. A dinner you and I are going to prepare. Right here in Nana's house, where those big family dinners all started. Grandma and Grandpa will come. So will Aunt Jo. And I'll bet I can get Uncle Tony to come, with a little persuasion, if I ask him myself. And I know that Rachel and Wally—"

"Yeah, yeah, yeah," said Aaron. "Get to the point. What about your father and Barbara?"

Her smile faltered.

"Sorry," he said, knowing how easily she was hurt on that particular topic. "But you've got to face reality on this one."

"I think they'll come." She said the words bravely. "Yes, they'll come," she reaffirmed. "They will." It was an act of pure, stubborn faith.

"You think your father will come to the house of a daughter he's all but banished? Not to mention knowing that his outcast brother Tony might be here, too?"

"My Dad has incredible social skills," said Gina. "There's no reason why he can't use those skills when dealing with members of his own family."

"And what about your grandparents?" said Aaron. "Does this mean you're going to tell them about the baby?"

"As soon as the holidays are over, there won't be a baby."

"You don't think your father will spill the beans?"

That warranted consideration. "You're right," she said. "It will come out. I don't want them to hear about it from Dad. I'll tell them myself. They'll still come."

"Gina, Gina, you can't be serious." Her plan was so full of loopholes that he didn't know where to start. "You're talking about cooking a major holiday dinner for how many?"

"Well, I guess there would be — let's see, nine, ten—"

"All by yourself?"

"By myself?" said Gina. "Nonsense! I've got a strong, handsome Jewish slave who obeys my every whim and does all the dirty work."

"Do I know this poor wretch?"

"You don't mind, do you?"

"Mind? Why should I mind? I'll have a ring-side seat when they tear each other apart."

She didn't seem to hear him. "I know exactly what I'll cook. Polenta, just like Nana used to make, and meatballs and hot sausages, and a big tub of moustaccioli, and I'll have Grandma show me how to make the sauce so it will be perfect."

"Your sauce will be perfect?" said Aaron. "Your pasta sauce won't matter, Gina. The dinner will be wasted. There'll be no one left alive to eat it."

"Very funny."

"Gina, be real. Your family will self-destruct in less than three minutes. Couldn't we play Russian roulette instead?

You want to have the mass slaughter of your blood relatives on your conscience?"

To his surprise, her face turned red, as though he'd slapped her. When she finally looked up at him, her eyes were bright with tears she refused to shed.

"I'm sorry," he said earnestly. "I wasn't thinking—"

"I know, I know."

She would never get over the shock and pain of her mother's death. He kissed a tear from her cheek.

"You can be witty and cynical, if you like," said Gina. "In fact, I find it very sexy." She kissed him back. "But you're wrong about this. I'm going to buy the invitations right now. I can get them written and in the mail before the last pickup."

"Invitations!" said Aaron. "In the mail!" Panic edged his voice. This wacky scheme was lurching toward reality at an uncomfortably rapid pace. "Please, Gina, now think about this. I mean, family squabbles sometimes just need time to heal. Give them a chance and everyone will do the right thing, sooner or later. You can't rush it by inviting every member of your hot-tempered family—"

"It's the right thing to do, Aaron." Gina rose to her feet, with a determined smile. "I know it is. Believe me."

He took her by the shoulders. "You're really ready to face your Dad?" he said quietly. "After the way he's treated you?"

This time her voice quavered, but her jaw tightened with resolution. "My Dad is hurting just as much as I am, Aaron. One of us has to make the first move. A big Christmas dinner is what this family needs. A dinner just like Nana used to cook."

CHAPTER EIGHT

Invitations

1
Return to the Past

Lou Rossi was sweeping off the porch when the postman stopped at the triplex. He didn't see the man coming up the stairs behind him because he was too busy remembering the terrible phone call yesterday, the news that had shattered their peaceful afternoon.

His granddaughter was pregnant. Unmarried, with child—

"Good morning, Mr. Rossi."

He looked up, startled to find himself no longer alone on the porch. He accepted the mail in the clumsy fingers of his gardening glove.

As the postman walked away, he recognized the handwriting on the envelope. So this was the other surprise his granddaughter had hinted at! He tore open the envelope, pulled out the invitation, and read it through.

The broom slipped out of his hands. It tumbled, banging and leaping, down the front stairs into the rhododendrons.

Lou scarcely noticed. He sat down abruptly on the top stair. He had to wait until his heart stopped hammering. Then he read the invitation again.

Christmas Eve. A family dinner at Nana's house. On that day, of all days!

Watching his granddaughter buy the house had been hard enough. But it hadn't stopped there. He'd had to go back to the house again and again, helping her bring the old place back to life. He'd endured it all for love of Gina. He'd almost gotten used to it. But now this.

A family dinner.

It wasn't the distant past that bothered him. Lou would have no trouble at all returning to the house of his boyhood. To the house he had lived in before the war, before the Navy, before his father's death. It was what the house had become that bothered him. The house where his mother had lived the rest of her life alone, until she could no longer be counted on to take baths or eat meals or find her way home from her far-ranging walks.

She had started forgetting to take her pills. She started getting on the wrong buses. She left her purse at the bus stop. She kept losing her groceries before she could get them home. One night she fell down the basement stairs. The next day he found her still lying on the basement floor, stretched helplessly on the cement for almost twelve hours.

It seemed like things couldn't get worse. And then things had gotten so much worse.

Near the end, on that last awful day, she had been watching for his arrival. He had glimpsed her briefly in one of the upstairs windows. She had fled at the sight of him.

Refusing to leave.

The memories wouldn't go away. He could still see her, his sobbing, protesting mother with her gray hair wild and undone, hiding from him upstairs, running from his approach, ignoring his calming words, his soothing promises.

How she had screamed and cried when he found her!

He had dragged her out of one hiding-place after another, torn her away from what was left of her life, ignored her shrieks of protest. Her loving son had condemned her to a nursing home full of strangers where she would quickly lose what was left of her memory as well as her will to live.

He stopped himself. He couldn't bear to remember any more. Lou loved his mother so much! He had tried to do the right thing. He would never know if he had.

He had spent the rest of the year going through her belongings, and then sold the house to Remedios Del Donno.

Two years later, at lunch with a realtor from Beacon Hill, Lou discovered that Mrs. Del Donno had tired of the house in an unusually short time. She had sold it to the gentleman next door, Walter Woo, whose extended family had grown too large, who welcomed a convenient addition to his own home.

Not convenient enough. In less than two years, it was sold again to Sokha Sok, who eagerly sold it to Gina. And so the house had strangely returned to the Rossi family.

2
Inescapable Burden

Stirring the chicken soup on the stove, Gloria Rossi heard her husband come in from sweeping the front stairs. She noticed that Lou was taking an unusually long time making his way down the hall.

He appeared in the kitchen doorway. She could tell from his expression that something had disturbed him.

"What's wrong now?" As if yesterday's upsetting phone call hadn't been enough!

"Take a look," he said, handing her the invitation.

Gloria held it up to the light, squinted at the squiggly lettering, and made out the words one by one.

"I don't believe it," she said slowly. "And in her condition! That girl is biting off more than she can chew. A huge mistake. You really think her father will come? You know Sam. Once he's lost his temper, he doesn't back down easily. And what about Tony? Not in a million years. She's dreaming if she thinks her Uncle Tony is going to come."

"Well, if she wants to do it," said Lou philosophically, "there's nothing we can do to stop her. She chose the perfect place to do it."

"The perfect place," she conceded to her husband.

She dropped the subject. Nana's death had not been particularly painful for Gloria. Her clinging, possessive mother-in-law had been the inescapable burden of her married life, the ever-present price of marrying Lou Rossi. The old woman's blind adoration of her only son had accorded Gloria the family status of favored servant. Nana's death had been a liberation, beginning the happiest seven years of Gloria's marriage. A Christmas Eve dinner at Nana's house sounded like a nightmare.

And she dreaded the effect it would have on her husband. The harrowing experience of taking care of his mother those last few years, stopping by her house every morning before work, every evening after work, watching her forget more and more, had drained him, aged him. She didn't want to watch Lou go through all that again.

Lou and Gloria regarded each other. They didn't have to talk about it.

"Well, one thing's for sure," said Gloria. "Gina will need some help. Sounds like you and I are going to be busy."

"She'll never be able to do it alone," he said. He scowled at the invitation. "Dinner doesn't start until eight. Seems pretty late for Christmas Eve." He pointed out the number to his wife. "Can you see this? Is that an eight or a three?"

"Looks like a three to me," said Gloria. She squinted at it. "But I'm not wearing my glasses."

3

Complication

Barbara Rossi checked the casserole in the microwave. She was throwing together something quick for Sam and the kids, before her meeting with the church charity drive committee.

She was an attractive woman in her late thirties with a distracted look in her dark eyes, as though she had succeeded in remembering many obligations, but had forgotten one important thing. Her kitchen windows looked out on well-kept gardens and lawns in a neighborhood of wealthy homes and curving, tree-lined streets. The kitchen was huge, with all the latest conveniences. She commanded it briskly and efficiently, and often at great speed. There was never enough time.

The telephone rang.

It was Sam, calling to say he'd be late for dinner. He was the kind of husband who was often late, and always called.

She was lucky. She had managed to marry the man of her dreams. Sam Rossi had given her everything she ever wanted — dream husband, dream kids, dream house. There was only one complication to her complete peace of mind, one lingering threat to her happiness and her family.

Her brother-in-law, Tony.

It wasn't that there was anything obviously wrong with Sam's brother. He just made her nervous. For one thing, when she looked him in the eye, she always suspected he might be on drugs. And whenever he got around her kids, and especially whenever she found him hanging around Wally, she got an uncomfortable shiver. What were his intentions? She, for one, could never forget what he had been accused of, not so long ago.

She had always made certain Uncle Tony was never alone with her attractive, lost, impressionable son. Wally was too vulnerable. She could scarcely conceal her relief when Sam and his brother began to see less and less of each other. Uncle Tony hadn't come to a family dinner for years. She liked it that way.

The microwave bell dinged. Her casserole was ready. She wouldn't have time to eat any. She was already going to be a few minutes late to her meeting.

She was quickly chopping some nuts for the topping when Wally shuffled in after school, mumbled hello, and dropped the mail on the kitchen table. With the phone propped between her shoulder and ear, she nudged aside the bills, uncovered the holly-bordered envelope, noticed who it was from, and tore it open.

Sam was just getting ready to hang up. She didn't let him.

"Guess what arrived in the mail today—"

4

The Subject Is Closed

Traffic was hell.

Interstate-5 was backed up like a sewer. Afternoon rush hour had tied up all lanes. Christmas made it worse. There was obviously an accident up ahead somewhere. He just couldn't see where. All Sam Rossi could see were cars and cars and cars, slowing down all around him into a thick, metal mess.

He would clearly not be home in time for dinner. He reached for his car phone, keeping an eye on the nervous, indecisive driver on his right.

"Hi, honey," he said. "Hey, I'm doing my best, but it's not good enough."

Sam Rossi always did his best. Lately his best had not been good enough. After trying to be a good person, a good Catholic, and a good parent for almost twenty years, he now found himself not speaking to his brother and on terrible terms with all three of his children.

His oldest daughter had gotten herself pregnant. His second daughter was violently rejecting Catholicism. And his son, his greatest hope, had turned his back on sports, had dropped off the basketball team and the baseball team and the soccer team, and why? So that he could waste his time drawing cartoons. For Sam Rossi, all three of his greatest investments in life had gone belly up.

Sam would never reveal his growing sense of unhappiness to anyone. He never showed his loved ones the chinks in his armor. He showed his love in his strength, in his ability to protect and provide. In his control.

"Thanks for calling, sweetheart," she said. "Love you."

"Love you." It was formula, but true. He did love his wife. She was smart, pleasant, gorgeous, a great mother, an armful in bed, a social ally, a reliable friend.

"Take your time," she said. "Tonight's my charity drive meeting, remember? I made a casserole for you and the kids."

"Sounds great. See you soon."

She surprised him by staying on the line. "Guess what arrived in the mail today."

Sam edged around a semi-truck that was blocking his vision, and began watching for an opportunity to slip into the next lane. "More bills," he said.

"Of course, more bills," said Barbara. "That's a law of the universe. There are always more bills. Besides those."

"I give up," said Sam. He saw his chance. He was a good driver. He made his move, and was in the next lane, smooth and easy. "Tell me. What came?"

"An invitation," said Barbara. "From Gina."

He stopped seeing the freeway lanes ahead of him. He was seeing his daughter's face. Gina. A very painful subject. What was it about her that made him love her so much he ended up shouting? He tried to hear what Barbara was saying.

"—a Christmas Eve dinner in her new home. For the whole family."

"Christmas Eve?" said Sam. "The whole family? Well, that's her stupidest move yet. I shudder to think what the next stunt will be. Obviously, we're not going to any such dinner. The subject is closed."

"I wouldn't be so sure about that," said Barbara skeptically.

"The subject is closed," he repeated with fervor. Sam Rossi gripped the steering wheel. He meant it. He was in control.

5
Smoke Gets in Your Eyes

The kitchen table was floating in a linoleum sea.

Wally Rossi could feel the linoleum rising, sinking, causing his chair to surge and fall, bobbing on waves of plastic yellow. He gripped the edge of the kitchen table, feeling the floor heave and sink below him.

It was no accident that Wally's baseball cap was tipped strategically forward. The brim of the cap, at that particular angle, effectively concealed his red eyes from his mother.

Not that hiding anything from his mother was so hard to do. Mom always had other things on her mind. At the moment, she had effectively forgotten that her son was even there. Which was fine with Wally.

Mom was getting pretty worked up over something with his father on the phone. Something about a disaster being planned by his sister on Christmas Eve.

"You may consider the subject closed," said his mother, "but is that what you're telling your parents? Is that what you're tellingl your kids? I think not, dear. I think you may not realize it yet, but you've just had your Christmas Eve plans decided for you, whether you like it or not."

Wally listened intently, not budging an inch for fear of betraying his presence.

He was a shy, pudgy fourteen-year-old who preferred reading comics to playing on a Little League team. He'd tried to please his Dad. He'd turned out for every sport. He'd always been mediocre, and hated every minute of it. He would rather read an exciting book than play on any team. He would rather watch a movie than a football game. Instead of a national sports logo, his baseball cap featured Mickey Mouse. His sweatshirt proudly displayed Sylvester the cat and Tweetie.

Wally loved cartoons. He had a passion and talent for drawing. He sketched cartoon characters all up and down the margins of his notebook paper. He did caricatures of his teachers and many of his classmates. Someday he would create a great comic strip. Meanwhile, life was hell.

Six months ago, Wally Rossi had shared a joint with a neighborhood kid in the park. Wham. He had discovered a whole new planet. He wasted no time returning again and again to the exhilarating world of stoned fantasies. His parents didn't suspect a thing. He got high during his lunch breaks. It was easier to get through school that way. He didn't have to worry about what the other kids thought of him. He was safe in his own world.

Not until his mother was hanging up the phone did she see Wally in front of her, sitting at the kitchen table, clearly listening to every word.

"Getting an earful?"

He grinned and nodded. By now he knew all about his half-sister Gina's Christmas Eve dinner.

"And what exactly is on your mind, mister?"

"Not much," said Wally. That was his new answer. And it summed up how much his mother knew about him these days.

He made a move toward the hall door.

"Just a minute, young man," said Mom, setting down the hot casserole on the counter. She regarded him swiftly with a sharp, practiced eye. "Why do those eyes look so tired? Are you getting enough sleep?"

"Sure, Mom. Guess I better start on my homework."

He bounded up the stairs two at a time, cut a sharp turn down the hall, darted into his bedroom, and slammed the door. Made it! His gecko stared at him out of the glass terrarium. He gave a few friendly taps on the glass with his fingernail. The gecko blinked at him.

He pulled out his sketchbook, stretched out on the bed, and returned to work on his exciting new comic-strip. Stroke by stroke, frame by frame, his pencil brought to animated life the incredible heroic exploits of Super Gecko, Master of the Universe.

Christmas Eve at Nana's house, he thought. Well, things could be worse. His memories of Nana's house were vague, but he seemed to remember lots of rooms upstairs. Plenty of places to disappear to, if the scene became too intense. Places where no one would find him if he needed to calm down.

Because he intended to remain calm. He would be bringing both his sketchbook and something to smoke to Christmas Eve dinner.

CHAPTER NINE

The Unknown

1
The Bedroom Window

From the moment she dropped the invitations into the mailbox on Beacon Avenue, Gina began acting as though her frightening experience in the little staircase had never happened.

Aaron wasn't fooled. He tried not to make it obvious how closely he was watching her. She had no idea how often his eyes looked up over the edge of his organic chemistry textbook. Her hysterical state when he found her trapped in that closet had unnerved him. He had never seen her so frightened. She was still a mystery to him in so many ways. He slipped into bed beside her that night and watched her sleep. So beautiful, so unknown.

What could have happened to her? What had really frightened her?

He waited until the following day, after Gina was thoroughly rested, when she had regained her cheer and energy and looked ready to face her fears. "Feel like going back upstairs for another look in that closet?"

Gina visibly tensed. "I suppose that's a good idea," she said. "It would be pretty silly to be scared of going into your own closet, wouldn't it?"

Together they returned to the room at the end of the east hall. Aaron walked beside her, letting her clutch his hand. Sunlight spilled through the windows into the open closet. It looked big and empty and harmless.

Aaron walked ahead of her down the length of the closet. When he pushed open the little door, he saw her take an unintentional step backward.

"No, thanks," she said. "That staircase is a little tight for my taste. Maybe tomorrow. You go, if you want to."

He disappeared up the stairs.

He came down laughing.

"I know what you heard," he said. "And it wasn't the ghost of Nana, because I just heard it, too. We've got boarders. There are some pigeons nesting under the eaves."

"Pigeons?" said Gina.

"You can hear them cooing through the wall."

"It wasn't pigeons."

He grinned at her. "They're pretty noisy birds."

Was she really so sure? A simple spell of dizziness and a bang on the head could so easily have combined to become a supernatural experience.

He kissed her. "Italians are so dramatic," he said. "This house is a little spooky sometimes, that's all. It's just old. We'll soon be used to every creak and groan."

She smiled. She seemed to be listening to him. Then she said, "I wonder if they'll get their invitations today."

"Probably tomorrow," said Aaron.

"Good," she said. "They'll come, Aaron. Even my Dad. You watch. I know they'll come."

"That's what I'm afraid of," he muttered.

She didn't hear him. She seemed quite confident about it all, back in the real world again. Together they left the closet behind and returned downstairs. It became understood between them, without either speaking a word, that her ghostly experience in the odd little staircase wouldn't be mentioned again.

*

"See something interesting?"

He wrapped his arms around her from behind. She hadn't heard him enter, yet she wasn't startled at all. She almost seemed to be waking up.

Aaron was fresh from outside, still wearing his winter jacket, cheeks flushed, backpack full of textbooks. He had bussed home early from campus. He found Gina in their bedroom, her back to the door, standing motionless in front of the glass. A bottle of Windex and a soggy, darkly-smudged paper towel lay on the windowsill beside her, but she was no longer cleaning the glass. She was simply staring out the window, as though something in the garden below were the most interesting thing on earth.

His voice seemed to snap her out of it.

"Oh! Hi, there. You caught me daydreaming." She turned around in his arms and smiled up at him.

"Is that what you call it?" he said. "Confess. What you were really doing was thinking about what you're going to plant down there in that cute little vegetable garden."

She kissed him lightly on the nose.

"You know me too well."

*

That night Aaron rolled over in bed and discovered a stretch of cold sheet where he had expected to find Gina. He was surprised enough by his discovery to wake up. The room was too dark to see much, but he could make out a figure standing before the window, bathed in moonlight.

"Gina?"

She didn't hear him.

He slipped out of bed and stepped toward her, barefoot, over the cold wood floor.

"Gina, are you okay?"

She didn't seem to realize he was there. She was staring out the window again, the same way he'd found her that afternoon, her features silver with moonlight, her eyes intently searching for something in a dreamworld fog. He came up beside her, put his arm around her shoulders.

"What is it? What's wrong?"

"Aaron?" She looked confused. She blinked at the window where she found herself, at the bed where she should have been. "I couldn't — I couldn't sleep, that's all."

"Come on back to bed."

"It's so cold." She shivered.

"I'll warm you up," he said. "Get back under the electric blanket where you belong."

2
The Man Who Vanished

She remembered kissing Aaron good-bye at some vague, pleasant moment during the early morning hours, just before he left for classes.

Shortly after lunch, Gina thought she heard someone in the backyard, but then the garbage truck rumbled through the alley, which explained that.

She had not been aware of anyone lurking about the house when she went down to check the mailbox. She had found two bills waiting for her. She had opened and gasped over the heating bill as she walked back up the porch stairs. If anyone had been loitering about the house, she might not have noticed.

She might not have known that he was there at all, if she hadn't decided to empty the garbage. Out the kitchen door she went, through the tight confines of the back porch and down the back stairs, following the path around the red-brick corner of the house.

She stopped abruptly in her tracks. He was slumped over outside the basement door, curled up like a homeless man trying to get warm, occasionally making wet, snuffling sounds.

A faded, black stocking-cap swallowed up most of his head. It was covered with fuzzballs. The knees of his dirty, black Levi's were folded up to his stubbled chin. The worn-out elbows of his old green parka poked out from the arms wrapped around his legs. He rocked back and forth just slightly. His head, nestled between his arms, made sad, wheezing sounds which caused his shoulders to tremble.

He raised his head.

His eyes were wet and red and puffy. At first she didn't recognize him. It had been so many years since she had last seen him.

"Uncle Tony?"

"Hi, Gina." He sniffed noisily.

Throughout Gina's childhood, family dinners for the holidays had revolved every year from house to house, sometimes with her Mom and step-father in Tacoma, sometimes with her Dad and Barbara, sometimes at Grandma and Grandpa's, sometimes at Nana's. But for some reason, family dinners never happened at Uncle Tony's apartment.

Of course, Uncle Tony didn't have a wife to do the cooking. But everyone said he was a great chef. So, why not?

Gina took a step toward him, cautious not to crowd him. "Are you okay?"

"I'm okay," he said. He sniffed. He smiled weakly.

That smile. How she had loved her uncle, how she had missed him!

So, why did no one ever go inside Uncle Tony's apartment? He lived at the top of three flights of stairs, and was always waiting on the porch to spot the car picking him up. Gina, Rachel and Wally had been intensely curious about the house no one entered. As kids they used to hotly compete to see who could get up the stairs first to help Uncle Tony carry down his Christmas presents. Because whoever did might get a glimpse inside.

Once Gina succeeded.

Someone else was there, too. He didn't approach or talk to her. He was much younger and nice-looking and not wearing a shirt. A few years ago Gina had put all those ingredients together into a new understanding of her uncle.

"Are you cold?"

"No, I'm fine." He wiped his nose on his sleeve. "I'm fine. I'm just sad."

When had she last seen him? The first absences seemed so natural. She didn't realize that the excuses were never going to end. Uncle Tony had missed so many holiday dinners that no one expected him anymore. At the last Christmas dinner before leaving for Notre Dame, in front of everyone at the table, Gina had surprised and embarrassed her father by announcing how much she missed her uncle.

Her Dad's response had been so startling and unexpected she never forgot it.

"You miss your Uncle Tony? You don't remember him enough to miss him. Because there's nothing to miss. He can't hold a job longer than a year. He's got no wife. No kids. No car. No career. No television. No bankcard. Not even a business suit. You can define my dear brother by what he doesn't have. I doubt if you'll be seeing too much of your Uncle Tony anymore."

And now, here he was.

She was hesitant to approach any closer. He looked scruffy and ill-kept, his cheeks unshaved. The heels of his weather-beaten shoes were gouging holes in her garden-bed. But the eyes. They were Uncle Tony's eyes. Eyes she had trusted for as long as she could remember. Impulsively, she dropped down beside him and embraced him.

"It's so good to see you again, Uncle Tony."

"You, too, Gina."

He was two years older than her father, but had always acted younger. He had a hearty laugh that was slightly too loud and friendly eyes that seemed to be aware of a private joke. Those eyes were messy now with emotion.

"I got your invitation," he said, sniffing. "I had to come and see the old house for myself."

"Well, I'm happy you did," said Gina. "Why are you crying, Uncle Tony?"

"Oh, don't mind me," he said. "I'm the emotional one in the family, remember? It's just being here, seeing this place again. Nana was such an incredible woman. She played a pretty big role in my life, honey. She had a heart as big and as crazy as this whole house."

"Well, the house is just as big and crazy as ever," said Gina. "Except that now it's mine. Want to see it?"

"Could I?" His smile brightened. He clambered up onto his feet, brushing himself off.

Gina was delighted. "Let me give you the grand tour."

3
Guilty

Uncle Tony surprised her by giving her a tour just as grand. A tour of the past. With each room that she showed him, he supplied remembered stories and details to give her a glimpse into another room that was no longer there.

"This is Aaron's study."

"So I see. This used to be Grandpa's bedroom, when he was a kid. Then your Dad and I used to sleep here, whenever the two of us spent the night at Nana's."

She continued on to the next door. "And this is our room."

"It was Nana's bedroom, too. Oh, my God. That picture." A huge framed wedding portrait of a handsome young Italian couple, Orsola and Niccolo Rossi, hung over the four-poster bed. "That incredible picture. Where'd you get it?"

"From Grandpa."

"It's so good to see it again." He choked on his words. "Don't mind me. Really. Stuff about Nana always makes me emotional. Her love was so strong, Gina. She loved me more than any human being alive."

"I only wish I could have known her better," said Gina. She waited for him to swipe at his wet eyes with the back of his knuckles. She took her uncle's hand, and led him down the hall and around the corner.

Uncle Tony stopped abruptly.

"I remember this door," he said. "It leads to the stairs that go up to the second floor."

"You know this house better than I do."

"Oh, I remember those stairs. We used to play up on the second floor with our cousins. Scary games in the dark. I didn't like it upstairs. I used to get too scared. There are two halls, right? The east hall and the west hall. Three rooms on this side, three rooms on that side."

"Same number I came up with, the last time I counted," said Gina. "Want to take a peek?" She opened the door wider. Her uncle poked his head cautiously over her shoulder. "Go on. No one's going to bite you."

He laughed and backed nervously away. "No, thanks. I used to get too scared up there as a kid. Bad memories. Some other time."

*

Not until Uncle Tony had a chance to wash his face and freshen up in the bathroom, not until they were both laughing and comfortable in the breakfast nook, poking at the crumbs of the remaining peach cobbler and sipping at steaming mugs of coffee, did Gina finally ask her uncle the question she hadn't dared to ask.

"Why did you disappear, Uncle Tony?"

He paused, his mug midway to his lips. "You mean, you don't know? My brother didn't tell you?"

"Dad said you two had a disagreement. That's all he would ever say. You know Dad."

"They never told you about me, huh? Not even your Mom or Barbara?"

"Mom didn't talk about the Rossi family," said Gina. "And you know Barbara. She's a Dad-supporter, one hundred percent. What didn't they tell me, Uncle Tony?"

There had always been a mysterious strain and hesitation whenever her adult relatives talked about her uncle. Their voices became softer and softer, the closer any young person got to the conversation, so that Gina could never hear exactly what they were saying.

"They didn't tell you," said her uncle, "that I was accused of something awful."

"Something awful? No, Uncle Tony."

"I was accused—" His lower lip trembled in a weird, sad way. "—the family who brought the charge against me said that I sexually molested their seventeen-year-old son."

"You what?" said Gina.

It came out of nowhere. How could her parents have managed to keep something as big as that out of her hearing? She looked into her uncle's eyes. He was scrutinizing her reaction, watching her every move in terrified fascination, ready to spot the first sign of doubt, of distrust.

92

Gina could see what was needed, and immediately hugged him. She clutched him, and didn't let go until he stopped being stiff, until he relaxed and put his arms around her. "Oh, Uncle Tony, what a horrible lie! Why would anyone say that?"

"A very disturbed and lonely kid said that," said Tony. "He was confused and afraid of himself and tremendously angry. And everyone in my family who should have known better, who should have believed me, believed him."

"Not everybody," she objected.

"They all secretly thought I was guilty. They would never admit it, but they did. They all wondered if maybe I did molest teenage boys."

"Nobody thought that!" denied Gina.

"Everybody thought that. Didn't you notice that all of a sudden I was never left alone with you kids? Well, believe me, I noticed. After a couple weeks, the kid confessed. He admitted he was lying. But no one ever forgot what he said. It's still there. And I can't forget that my own family didn't trust me."

"I've always trusted you, Uncle Tony," began Gina, but that was all the farther she got.

Thong—

That sound again. From somewhere upstairs. The rubbery thud she'd heard in the closet staircase. Uncle Tony didn't seem to hear it.

Thong—

"What's wrong?" asked Uncle Tony.

"Didn't you hear anything?"

A shattering crash directly above them.

Silence.

Uncle Tony rose slowly to his feet. "I heard that." His face drained of color, his eyes widening. "Is someone else here besides us?"

"Of course not," said Gina.

"Well then, who—?"

She laughed nervously. "No need for alarm. I've been moving things around upstairs. Obviously something wasn't as balanced as I thought."

He tried to laugh, too. "Obviously." He shrugged, edgy, unconvinced. "Well, it sure has been great seeing you. I suppose I should probably be on my way."

"How did you get here, Uncle Tony?"

"On the bus. And that's exactly how I'm going home."

"Let me give you a lift."

"Nonsense. Good-bye, I'm off."

"Wait, not so fast. You're coming to my Christmas Eve dinner, I hope?"

"Oh, now Gina. I'm sorry but I can't actually—"

"You've got to."

"Gina, really, I would but—"

"I'm begging you, Uncle Tony."

"You would never ask that of me, would you? Surely you don't expect me to face my brother?"

"If I can face my father," said Gina, "why can't you face your brother? They're both the same person."

He looked at her with sympathy. "You two not seeing eye to eye?"

"You know what he's like," said Gina. "Please, Uncle Tony, you've got to come."

He sighed. "All right, all right. If you insist—"

"I absolutely insist."

"I give up. I accept your invitation." He rose to his feet with a groan. "If you're determined to celebrate Christmas Eve at Nana's house—" He shuddered. "—I'll be there."

4
Rubber Ball

Her uncle slipped out the back door as though he were slipping out of her life. She watched through the small window over the kitchen sink as his stocking-capped head bounced down the back stairs. She caught a glimpse of him as he cut across the lawn toward Beacon Avenue and the bus stop, his hands shoved down into his pockets, his shoulders hunched against the cold.

She wondered if she would ever see him again. She watched until he was out of sight. Then she listened.

A tense silence.

What in the world could have fallen? She wracked her memory, trying to think of what she had piled on what. Nothing particularly risky or unstable. It had all seemed secure at the time. Clearly something had not been.

She hesitated. She didn't particularly feel like going upstairs to find out.

"I don't believe it," she said to herself. "I refuse to be afraid in my own house."

She forced herself to cross the kitchen, walk down the hallway, and open the door to the staircase. She listened.

Nothing.

There was no avoiding going up there and finding out the bad news. She couldn't just ignore it.

She remembered the scattered bursts of footfalls she and Aaron had heard on Thanksgiving. The thought gave her a chill of fear. What if whatever-it-was had come back?

Gina stepped up the first two stairs and stopped. She peered into the darkness at the top of the staircase. Nothing but motionless shadows, where the east hall and west hall both came to an end.

She quietly stepped up one more stair. One more. She stopped and listened.

Thong—

Gina froze. She held her breath, listening intently.

Thong—

She looked up the staircase before her.

A child's red rubber ball, the size of an apple, came bouncing slowly down the stairs toward her, impossibly slowly, as though in a dream.

*

"How's your head?"

Gina grimaced, holding the dripping icepack against the bump on her forehead. They were sitting together on the two bottom stairs of the staircase. "Throbbing."

"I didn't think you were the fainting type."

"I'm not."

"I'm getting scared to leave you alone when I go to class."

"Aaron, do you realize, that red rubber ball—"

"Oh, come on, Gina. No more about that ball. I tell you, there is no ball."

"Aaron, there most definitely was a ball, and it looked like an old ball. It must have belonged to Grandpa."

"Your grandfather?" he said. "How could it? Why would it still be here in the house after all the other owners? Where did this strange ball come from?"

"It's the sound I've been hearing. That thudding sound. A ball. Which explains the crash. The ball must have knocked over something upstairs. Aaron, you've got to believe me."

"Well then, where is this ball now?"

Gina groaned and clutched the ice-pack to her forehead. "I was in no condition to notice where the ball ended up. It has to be here somewhere."

"But it isn't. That's the problem, Gina. I've looked everywhere. There's no ball."

"There was a ball. A red rubber ball. It was real, Aaron. I know it was real. I saw it."

CHAPTER TEN

The Haunted

1
The Second Dream

"Can't sleep, can you?"

She had slept too much, that was the problem. Ever since her fall on the stairs, Gina had slept through the night and all the next day, in bed, in her reading-chair, on the sofa, wherever she happened to be, dropping off into deep blackout doses of unconsciousness. Now that night had come again, she was finally starting to wake up.

She had been stiff and restless ever since she laid down, keeping to her side of the bed. He could see that something was gnawing at her.

"I don't know what's wrong with me," she said, staring wide-eyed up at the shadowy ceiling. "I'm exhausted. I want to sleep. I'm trying very hard to sleep. My eyes just won't seem to close."

"Hmmmm," he said thoughtfully. "As a medical student, of course, I recognize the symptoms."

"You do?"

"It's a classic case." He kissed her on the forehead. "You've got too much on your mind. Well, don't you worry." He slid out from under the blanket. "Doctor Steiner can help you."

Suddenly she found herself in bed alone. She could hear his bare feet slapping across the floor.

"Yes, the good doctor himself is going to fix you a little sleeping potion he learned in chemistry class."

97

His voice trailed off down the hallway. She raised her head from the pillow and looked after him. Through the bedroom doorway she could see a sudden spill of brightness into the hall, as Aaron turned on the bathroom light. She sank back down into her pillow. She thought she heard the squeak of the medicine cabinet door.

*

It's that magic weekend again.

It's the one weekend in their lives that five-year-old Gina and eighty-eight-year-old Nana will ever spend alone together, the one time Gina will ever get to stay overnight at Nana's house for two days in a row.

It's a sunny afternoon. Gina's Mom and her stepfather have flown off to Cape Cod, and her Dad and Barbara have just driven away to catch a plane to Maui. Gina is suddenly free of all parents.

She and Nana are alone, just the two of them, with hundreds of flower-gardens and a house with a thousand rooms.

Gina is giddy with happiness on such a bright, cheerful day, and is following Nana around the side of the house. Her small hands are swallowed up in gardening gloves which are much too big, but which she prizes proudly, trying to work the fingers. She is clutching a small shovel. She is about to be initiated into the secrets of the plant kingdom.

Together they enter the vegetable garden.

It's a thriving, leafy jungle, row after row all heavy with harvest, beans and peas and ears of corn, fat squashes and long zucchinis. Nana stops to pick a raspberry from the prickly, berry-studded arbor.

"Open wide," she says to Gina.

Just as she is about to pop the ripe, red berry between her granddaughter's lips, Gina hears something. Something that frightens her.

Thong—

She would run, but her feet won't budge.

Thong—

Gina forgets all about the berry. She turns in circles in the garden, listening, searching in every direction. She notices a window high overhead. Something moves in the window. Something falls. And then she hears another mysterious sound, a sound that makes her cold inside.

"What is that, Nana?"

"Don't be scared." Nana tries to smile reassuringly. "It's just the wind."

But Gina knows her great-grandmother too well. She can see a frightened look in her eyes. She's lying. It isn't the wind.

That's the sound of a child crying.

*

Gina opened her eyes.

For a moment, she thought she could still hear the crying. It wasn't the child, at all. It was the wind. The cold night wind on her bare legs.

She didn't know where she was. The only light came from a distant streetlamp, illuminating part of an alley wall. Alley? Garbage can. Compost pile.

She was standing in the remains of the vegetable garden, in the middle of the night.

Her mouth opened in silent disbelief and shock. She was supposed to be in bed. She was supposed to be sleeping next to Aaron, with a warm electric blanket wrapped around them both. She was alone in her nightgown, clutching a shovel. A shovel? Where did the shovel come from? She'd seen one down in the basement, along with a rake and hoe, but—

She looked behind her. The darker shadow of the house loomed over her. Light spilled out through the open basement door. In turning around to face the house, she stepped to one side. The splash of light from the basement spilled across the garden. It revealed the overturned earth in front of her, sliced up in clumps, piled next to the beginnings of a shallow hole.

She had been digging.

Was she losing her mind? Gina became very afraid that she might be. Why would she be digging in the garden in the middle of the night?

Aaron was running toward her. The moment she felt his arms around her, she started to cry in sheer confusion.

"Gina, what is it?"

"I — I don't know."

"Come on back inside. It's freezing! Are you okay? What are you doing out here?"

"I don't know."

She wanted to answer him. She was afraid that if she tried, she wouldn't be able to stop crying. She allowed him to put his arm around her, to guide her toward the house.

"Aaron," she managed at last, as he closed and locked the basement door behind them, "am I — am I—?" She swallowed and tried again. "Do you think I'm going crazy?"

He hugged her. "Of course not! Gina, you're a rock of sanity. A little sleepwalking doesn't mean you're crazy. A lot of women do wilder things than sleepwalk when they get pregnant. It affects your mind, too, your thoughts, your emotions, your sleep, everything."

She began trembling uncontrollably.

2
At the Last Minute

"You're out of bed," he said as he entered the bedroom. "How do you feel?"

"Fine." That was all. As though nothing had happened last night. "I've been thinking about sunflowers," she added, looking down into the vegetable garden. "I'm going to plant a row of sunflowers along the back fence."

"Just like Nana did?" guessed Aaron, coming up beside her, studying her face in concern.

She smiled. "Just like Nana."

He kissed her on the cheek. "You must be starved. How about some lunch? You slept right through breakfast."

"You didn't go to classes!" she realized in sudden alarm.

"I had plenty of homework to do right here," he said, "where I could keep an eye on my friend."

He took her gently by the arm and led her away from the bedroom window, down the hall to the breakfast nook. Lunch exhausted her. She managed to decorate the mantelpiece with angel hair and holly sprigs, before taking a catnap on the sofa that unexpectedly lasted right through dinner.

*

By the following day Gina seemed stronger, but she was no longer quite so spontaneous, so willing to laugh. She was no longer sure what was real. Her whole sense of what she could believe about herself had been shaken. She was on guard, alert for any sign of irrational behavior.

Thoroughly rested, she was back on her feet, but only by purposely not thinking about her mysterious visit to the garden at night, or the red rubber ball that vanished, or the figure she'd seen in the closet stairway, or the bursts of running footfalls upstairs. Those inexplicable terrors were firmly walled out of her mind. She pretended they never happened.

All she allowed herself to think about was the family dinner. Each of the last dwindling days before Christmas had its agenda, its shopping list, its decoration countdown. Not to mention the things she kept adding at the last minute.

"Aaron, I just thought of something—"

Suddenly, out of nowhere, on the day before Christmas Eve, she realized that the final touch to lift everyone's expectations and brighten their memories of Nana's house would be Christmas lights. The missing ingredient! And not just a few lights. All around the front porch. All along the eaves. All around the windows. All around the house.

"Christmas lights?" he had echoed incredulously, as they sat together over the breadcrumbs of half-eaten sandwiches and half-empty bowls of tomato soup. "Now?"

Now, when the season was almost over, with only one day left before the commercial blitz of department stores gone crazy and electrified shopping malls finally fizzled out. Far too late in the holiday season for anyone in his right mind to be up on a ladder against the side of the roof, stringing long, loopy, tangled wires of Christmas lights along the gutters and eaves and windows of the house.

Gina looked him straight in the eyes. "There's still time," she said. "And it'll make such a huge difference. I'll be right back." She put on her coat, walked out the kitchen door, and drove away.

Ever since that night in the garden, something in Gina remained slightly aloof. At first he thought she was simply embarrassed to have fallen on the stairs or been caught sleepwalking. Or perhaps frightened by the incidents, scared that something like that might happen again. Now, however, she acted as though she were keeping a secret.

Aaron was out on the front lawn, raking up a few late-falling leaves, when she drove up an hour later. As she walked toward the house, her arms were so full he could hardly see her face. Boxes were piled up to her nose.

Christmas lights.

"Want a little help?"

"I can manage, thanks," she said. "But there's another load in the trunk. Can you get those?"

He did so, and piled his boxes next to her boxes on the front porch. "All these lights must have cost a fortune."

"What are MasterCards for?"

"But how can you afford to spend so much—"

"On sale for half-price. Will you help me hang them?"

"Of course, I will. There's a ladder in the basement. But you aren't getting up on any ladders until you feel better. Don't worry about a thing. You want Christmas lights, you got Christmas lights. This place is going to look classy."

"Classy traditional," qualified Gina. "Nothing too crazy. Something that will impress my family."

"Mission impossible," grumbled Aaron.

"Now, that's not fair," she snapped. "Come on, give them a chance."

"Okay, okay." He gave her a quick peck on the cheek. "How about this, for a basic light-hanging scheme?" He spread his arms dramatically to illustrate. "How about if I run them straight along the gutter in front, and then down around the two front windows, and then—"

She hadn't been listening to a word he said. She'd been worrying again. Would this go right? Would that go right? Would everything be exactly perfect for her wonderful, perfect family?

"Relax," he said. "Everything will be fine."

"I don't feel like relaxing. And everything has to be much more than fine."

"Hey, what you're doing this Christmas, it's already more than your dear family deserves."

"Aaron," she said firmly, "they're all I have left. Sometimes I may not act like it, but they're very important to me. I want to be part of this family. I want to *have* a family."

"You can have my family," said Aaron. "You can definitely have Aunt Miriam, and both of the Eisenbergs." His humor had no effect. "Listen, if the Rossis can't appreciate all the effort you put out for them, let them go to hell."

"Aaron!" Gina elbowed him in the side. "What a smart mouth you've got sometimes!"

"They don't deserve you," he persisted. "You love them so much, and you worry about pleasing them just right, and they treat you like dirt."

"You hurt me when you talk about them like that! You don't know them well enough to dislike them. You have no right."

"I do have a right," he countered. "I love you. That gives me the right."

"Oh, you don't understand." She turned away from him. "While you do the lights, I'm going to go buy another wreath for the other side of the fireplace. And I need more red bows. And another box of candles. And mistletoe. And a little more holly."

She left without another word, hurrying down the front porch steps toward the car.

103

She returned with every item.

From the moment she got home, she couldn't sit still, driven by some gnawing inner panic to make sure that every last detail about Christmas Eve was perfect.

She stepped outside to check on his progress. She remained to give him advice.

3
Christmas Lights

"How does it look now?"

"Crooked."

"Crooked? How can it still be crooked? I told you I'd never get it right," Aaron called down. "Jews were never intended to hang Christmas lights. It's not in my genes."

She ignored his attempt at humor.

"More this way," she called from below.

He leaned carefully to one side of the ladder, stretched out his arm, and tacked the string of lights into place.

"Anything you say," he mumbled.

This way, that way, it didn't matter to him. Anything to get it over with, and restore peace on the home front. The disturbing taste of their quarrel still lingered unpleasantly. A painful tension crackled between them.

"More to the left," she called from below the ladder.

He shifted the dangling wire of Christmas lights farther left along the gutter.

"Perfect," she called.

Nothing less than perfect for the Rossi family.

Just the back of the house left to do now. He descended and Gina helped him carry the ladder around to the backyard. He was hungry and cold and careful not to make any comment. The back of the house had been another issue. Why go through all the trouble? For the people who walk down the alley?

Her grandparents, she informed him, would park in back.

Fine. The back of the house would look beautiful, too.

Together they braced the ladder securely in front of the basement door, leaning it up against the windowframe of the master bedroom.

He made his way up each familiar rung of the old ladder, trailing one more looping string of Christmas lights behind him. It didn't take him long to tack it neatly into place along the back gutter.

"Perfect."

He was getting better at this. That left just the windows.

Gina reached up to him another dangling wire of lights. Bracing himself on the narrow brick windowledge, he lined the top of the master bedroom window. His nights in bed were about to be improved by the constant, irritating colored twinkle of Christian commercialism.

He kept his mouth shut. At least he was almost done. And not a minute too soon.

It was rapidly getting dark. Heavy clouds were bumping and shoving across the turbulent sky, and the wind was starting to get an icy edge. He could see the clouds reflected in the blackened glass of the bedroom window. Then he saw something more than reflected clouds.

He blinked.

What he saw was not in the sky. It was on the other side of the glass. A small round object.

Something that looked like a ball—

Bouncing through the open doorway. Bouncing across the bedroom. Bouncing directly toward him. Bouncing straight through the window, into his face. He almost lost his balance. He swatted in front of his eyes, as though beating away a pesty fly. Nothing there. Clutching the ladder, he looked down below.

Whatever it was, there was no sign of it now.

"Anything wrong?" asked Gina.

"I think I just got some dust in my eye."

"You okay?"

He blinked successfully. "Good as new."

Then he heard the crying.

The sound chilled him. He looked around for pigeons. There had to be pigeons! It seemed to be coming from the window. He could see something moving on the far side of the bedroom. What was that? He squinted through the glass. Something about two feet tall was moving toward him. Someone crouched over?

That unhappy crying sound.

Suddenly a face pressed up against the glass, looking out at him. A child's face. Then came the shriek, from somewhere behind the child.

Clutching the ladder, he jerked backward.

"Aaron, are you all right?"

Something fell off the windowledge on top of him. He thrust out an arm, to protect his face.

But his arm, quickly followed by his foot, had become entangled in the dangling Christmas lights. Aaron didn't realize he had lost his balance until he grabbed for the ladder to steady himself. His hand closed on air.

His arm, draped in glittering loops, swung out desperately, clawed at the gutter, and missed.

The last thing he heard was Gina screaming.

4
Tell Me What You Saw

"He's fine," she repeated to Grandma, as her grandfather handed her the phone to hear for herself. "No, he didn't break his leg. He fractured his left fibula and tore a couple tendons. He'll show you the splint. It's called an air cast. It's better for healing. It allows the foot muscles to move. You'll see it on Christmas Eve. Really, he's fine. It was very frightening but nothing permanent, nothing serious."

Nothing serious physically, maybe, but something had happened. Though neither of them would openly admit it, Aaron was acting like a stranger, hobbling around on his crutches, not looking her in the eye, refusing to talk about what happened up on the ladder.

She waited until that night, after dinner, after adjusting his blankets on the sofa to keep him warm and his foot uplifted, after tucking a steaming cup of raspberry tea within easy reach. He was staring at a sitcom on television, not responding to the one-liners, waiting out the laugh-track. Aaron hated sitcoms. Gina turned off the television.

"Does it hurt much?" she asked.

"The pain pills are taking care of it."

She curled up on the floor beside the sofa and took his hand. "When you go back to campus after Christmas, will you be able to get around on crutches?"

"I'll be fine. Don't worry."

"Aaron, tell me what you saw."

"I don't want to talk about it."

"It'll be good for you to talk about it."

"Not if I'm going crazy."

"But Aaron, I've seen things, too. What do you think happened to me in that staircase? I'll believe you. You don't have to convince me."

"Listen," said Aaron, "I'm a stressed-out med student. I had a dizzy spell on a ladder. Diagnosis: sleep deprivation. You, on the other hand, are going through a pregnancy. We're talking a whole major chemical and biological change, a psychological change."

"No," said Gina. "Be honest. We both know what's happening here. You're just afraid to say the word. I'll say it, and get it over with. We're talking about ghosts."

"Ghosts?" said Aaron, with a forced sound like a laugh. "Who's talking about ghosts? Is that what you're talking about?"

"We're both talking about ghosts," said Gina. "And we need to talk, Aaron. It's eating at both of us. The running footsteps. The crying. The red rubber ball. And remember how on Halloween you saw someone in the window? It's not just my imagination. We aren't alone in this house, Aaron. You know that as well as I do. There are others in this house. And not just one. More than one—"

"Not a chance," said Aaron. "Maybe you're talking about ghosts, but not me." He had no intention of telling her that he had seen the rubber ball. "I don't believe in ghosts. I believe in the real world. What I saw wasn't a ghost, it was more like — well, a reflection—"

"It wasn't a reflection."

"How do you know what I saw?"

"Aaron, if there's nothing strange in this house, then why do we both keep seeing and hearing things? How much longer can two sane people like us keep denying what we see and hear in our own house?"

He gave a nervous shudder and adjusted his splinted foot. "If you let yourself go," he said quietly, "you can start to believe anything. That can get pretty scary. So I say no to the whole thing. No ghosts! Because I want to stay sane. Either that, or I have to admit to myself that living here could be dangerous. Then it's time to start packing."

"Packing!" exclaimed Gina. "You'd just give up and leave?"

"Maybe we've just been lucky so far." He raised his splinted foot. "Maybe next time we won't be so lucky."

Her cheeks flushed red. She was on the edge of crying, but refused to let herself break down. "Well, of course, I understand. You're free to leave any time. This wasn't your idea, after all. But I'm not packing, Aaron. I won't leave. This is my home now. Nothing is going to drive me out of my home, nothing!"

CHAPTER ELEVEN

Family Dinner

1
Deadly Streets

Christmas Eve began as a bleak and unpromising morning. It was cold and wet, with a nasty wind and a sky that looked like it was darkening up for something really unpleasant.

The morning remained so dark it hardly seemed to happen at all, and then promptly lost all color and dissolved into white flurries of snow. Snow! Children cheered, adults groaned. A classic Christmas was in the making.

It was a white Christmas, all right, with a vengeance. The streets quickly became deadly. Radio announcers droned out warnings to everyone in the vicinity of Seattle. An accident here. An accident there. Traffic became a stalled and slippery nightmare. Neighbor skidded into neighbor, where icy driveway met icy street. Everywhere people were frantically sliding and falling through the red-and-green neon jungle toward home.

Shortly before noon, Grandma phoned. She was flustered and nervous. Conditions were getting worse.

"The north end is terrible," said Grandma. "I've never seen it snow so hard. How are things over there?"

"Beacon Hill isn't much better. I didn't realize it snowed like this in Seattle."

"The weather gets worse every year," said her grandmother. "Honey, I don't want to disappoint you, but I'm not so sure we're going to make it."

109

"Oh, Grandma!"

"Not in weather like this. It's just too dangerous. The streets aren't safe."

Five minutes after Grandma had hung up the phone, her gloomy withdrawal hovering in the air, Grandpa called.

"We'll be there," he said. "Don't worry."

"But Grandma said—"

"Your grandmother was just getting all worked up over nothing. You know how she gets when she's excited." Grandma had something to say about that in the background. Grandpa chuckled. "I know a way to avoid the hills. It may be a little slower, but it's perfectly safe."

"If you're sure, Grandpa," said Gina. "That would be wonderful. But I don't want you to drive if you don't feel comfortable."

"At our age," said Grandpa, "you never feel comfortable. We'll be seeing you soon. And don't worry about Uncle Tony. We're picking him up. He's right on the way."

"Thanks, Grandpa!" said Gina. "Drive really carefully. Promise?"

He promised.

2
Interrupted Kiss

"Well, how does it look?"

Flash! Gina smiled at the camera, surrounded by evergreen wreaths, red silk bows, and flickering Christmas candles.

The living room of Nana's house had been transformed into a tribute to the holidays of the Rossi past. A red ribbon had been hung across the top of the hearth, strung with half a dozen Christmas cards from friends and relatives. Photographs of the various Rossis, young and old, lined the holly-and-mistletoe-strewn mantelpiece. Most of the room was dominated by the tree, its huge branches laden with dozens of delightful ornaments. Brightly-wrapped presents, each topped with a gaudy bow, had been gathered under the winking, blinking colored lights.

"Like a real, old-fashioned Christmas," said Aaron behind the camera, stretched out on the sofa, his foot upraised on the armrest. "At least, that's how they are in the movies." He advanced the shutter. "Not that I'm any expert."

"Well, I know about Christmas," said Gina, "and I can tell you that—"

Flash! Another picture.

"Oh, Aaron, I wasn't even looking!" she scolded.

"I know," he said with a grin. "That's why I took it."

"Is that so?"

She leaned over and kissed him. He kissed her back. The kiss lingered, neither of them able to pull away. At least, not until the doorbell rang.

"Who could that be?"

"Who do you think," said Gina knowingly, brushing and patting herself back into respectability.

"But it can't be them already."

"Yes, it can. You know Grandpa."

"But I thought you said three o'clock. It's two-thirty."

"Merry Christmas, dear," she said. "Now, you stay right there and keep that foot up. I mean it. They won't be insulted." She hurried to open the front door.

3
Home Again

How strange the house looked, twinkling and sparkling with colored lights in all that blowing whiteness!

Lou could feel the blood pounding in his temples as he trudged through the snow from his parking place in back, the accordion case thudding and bumping against his ankles.

"Let me give you a hand with that, Dad," offered Tony.

Lou didn't need a hand, not with his accordion. "I've got it, I've got it. Help your mother with the presents."

Home again, for Christmas Eve!

They cautiously crunched their way up the snow-covered front stairs. Lou knocked. The front door swung open, and there was Gina, welcoming them into the decorated living-room of his mother's house.

"Merry Christmas!" They all said it at once.

"I know, I know," he said to Gina, "we're early." He was tipped sideways from the weight of the accordion. "But we wanted to leave enough time for the roads." He and Gloria were always teased about arriving long before anyone was ready for them.

"I'm exhausted," said Gloria. "That was the scariest ride of my life. It made me wish I was back in California."

Tony was shaved and tidy and wearing a nice sweater that was only slightly threadbare at the elbows. He looked nervous, and thoroughly uncomfortable. He hugged Gina, forcing a weak smile. "See, I told you I'd come."

Lou was choked with emotion, strangling on nostalgia but making a determined effort not to show it.

A row of big, red stockings hung from the mantelpiece, each one stitched with the name of a member of the family. Lou could remember when finding walnuts and an orange in his stocking was considered doing great. Candles and wreaths decorated each end of the fireplace, right where his mother always put hers. But Gina had gone even farther than that.

Lou leaned closer to one of the Christmas tree limbs and lifted up a fluffy white chain. His finger gently touched it. Popcorn. Strung popcorn.

He could remember his mother patiently sitting him down in the kitchen as a child, to teach him how to string popcorn. Slowly he had mastered using a needle and thread to produce a long, crackly chain. Twenty years later, he had watched her teach popcorn-stringing to his two sons, Tony and Sam. And twenty years after that, she had passed down that same art to her great-grandchildren.

Her great-granddaughter had remembered.

Home and yet not home. Other memories interfered. Later, troubled memories. The tragic last days of his mother's life. He distanced himself. It was no longer her house. It was somewhere else now, the home of his granddaughter.

"It looks wonderful, Gina," he said. "Just the way Nana would have liked it."

He kept an eye on his wife. Gloria was already in gear, and she could be very stubborn. She knew what she wanted. Family peace. From the moment she walked in, she was determinedly open-hearted and open-minded, ready to love everyone whether they wanted to be loved or not.

She made a bee-line for Aaron, greeting him as though he were a long-lost member of the family. Then she hauled her shy son, Tony, over to meet Gina's boyfriend, and left him there while she headed for the kitchen. Soon she was poking here, peeking there, checking to see how things were going. The first thing she did was inspect the sauce. She stirred it. She tasted it.

"What do you think?" asked Gina anxiously.

Gloria made a slight adjustment, a dash more of this or that.

Lou shook hands with Aaron, almost wished him a Merry Christmas, then clumsily substituted, "Happy Holidays." He examined the air cast. "Too bad about your foot."

Aaron made a dismissive sound. "It'll mend. Keeps doctors in business."

Lou strolled over to the television. "Mind if I turn it on? I just want to check the score."

"Go right ahead," said Aaron from the couch.

Anything to fill the awkward stillness, to help Lou get his thoughts away from that house. Every archway and windowsill assaulted him with memories. It was always so painful to remember how much he missed his parents. No matter how old he got, the pain never quite went away. And to be here in this house again on Christmas Eve, walking down these halls and looking through these windows—

"Did you see the game this morning?"

"I missed it. Who won?"

From his position on the sofa, splinted foot upraised, Aaron tried to engage Lou in light conversation. He made another friendly comment about football. Lou made one back. Soon they were making small talk with relative ease, while watching the football game.

Lou could see that his son, Tony, wasn't so lucky.

He hovered uncertainly, halfway between the laughing women in the kitchen and the men in front of the television. He didn't fit in either place. In frustration, he wandered aimlessly up one hall and down another, restless, anxious, through the kitchen and dining-room and back to the living-room, nervously awaiting the arrival of his brother.

The last anyone noticed, Tony had wandered up the staircase to the second floor.

4

What Happened Upstairs

A crash. The sound of something falling upstairs. Or someone.

They were all about to crowd up the stairs at once when the stairway door swung open and Uncle Tony lurched into the hallway. He looked disoriented. His face was pale.

"Uncle Tony, are you all right?" asked Gina in alarm.

"Fine, fine," he said. His voice was weak, the words lacked conviction.

"What happened?"

He pushed his way past them into the living-room, where he sank into the depths of an overstuffed armchair, clutching the armrests to steady himself.

"I tripped, that's all. I'm so clumsy. My feet just got tangled up."

"You've got to watch where you're going," scolded Gloria, her voice ringing through the dining-room from where she stood at the kitchen stove, eternally trying to force some sense into her son's thick head while continuing to stir the pasta sauce. "You've got to open your eyes. How can you be so smart and not see what's right in front of you?"

They all laughed.

Lou laughed, too. But something about Tony's story didn't ring quite true to him. He could see that familiar evasive look in his son's eyes. He seemed rattled, distracted.

"What's the matter?" asked Lou, nudging Tony.

"Nothing, nothing," said his son, nervously. "No, I'm fine, Dad, really. It's the memories, that's all. I'm sure it's even worse for you. Sometimes the memories seem so real that— " He tried to laugh it off, shrug it off. He didn't want to talk about it. He massaged his temples.

"Do you have a headache, Uncle Tony?" asked Gina. "Do you want some aspirin?"

"No, no, I'm fine," he said. "To tell you the truth, strange as it sounds, when I was upstairs just now — well, I heard this kind of weird thudding sound. I don't have a clue what it was. Spooked me." Another attempt to laugh it off. "And then, well— I could have sworn I heard someone crying."

He didn't notice the effect his words had on Gina, the abrupt tensing of her facial muscles, the widening of her eyes. Lou noticed.

Aaron looked away from the football game long enough to say, "You heard crying? The same thing happened to Gina. It's pigeons. They're nesting up against the house to keep warm." Aaron laughed, trying to make light of the matter. "It's just pigeons."

"Pigeons, huh?" said Uncle Tony, with as much belief as he could politely muster. "That's great. That's incredible. The sound was so human." He tried to shrug it off. "It must be nerves." Then he looked Gina in the eye. "You're nervous, too. Want to bet we're both nervous about the same thing?"

"Count me in, too," said Aaron.

The three of them shared in uneasy laughter.

"Just like old times," said Uncle Tony. "Everybody waiting for my brother to arrive."

The doorbell echoed through the house.

5
Uncomfortable Reunion

Gina opened the front door.

There stood her father, handsome and successful Sam Rossi, flanked by Barbara and Wally, all of them bundled up in bright plastic colors like a ski team, bearing armfuls of Christmas gifts equally colorful.

"Come in, come in." She quickly ushered them out of the cold. "It's so good to see you." She grabbed her half-brother. "Come here, you pest, give your sister a hug." She locked Wally in an affectionate wrestling hold. They jostled and tussled each other with rough, old-time intimacy. "Hi, Barbara." A graceful, restrained welcoming embrace, cheeks brushing in passing. And then there she was, face-to-face with her father.

"Well—" she began, and went completely speechless.

"Merry Christmas," he said, with an awkward grin.

"Merry Christmas to you, too." Gina was a nervous wreck. "Nice to see you, Dad." Their hug was strained. The bond was too flimsy yet, held together by nothing but good intentions. "Thanks for coming."

"I wouldn't have missed it for the world." The irony in his voice wasn't lost on her. Still, at least he was there. And now that he had successfully overcome one of his hurdles, he turned to face the other. "Merry Christmas, brother."

Uncle Tony nervously stepped forward.

The two brothers greeted each other as cheerfully as possible, almost hugging but not quite, shaking hands firmly if not warmly, acting as though the years of silence between them had never happened.

"Been a while."

"Sure has."

"It's about time," said Gloria bluntly from the kitchen doorway, continuing to stir the sauce.

Wally bounded impatiently forward. "Great to see you, Uncle Tony." He gave him a big hug. Wally had always

116

naturally gravitated toward him. Uncle Tony was the only one besides Rachel who had ever looked at his drawings and liked them, who had ever encouraged him to draw.

Barbara uneasily noticed her son's attraction to his uncle. She tried not to show that she was watching them. She smiled warmly at her brother-in-law, embraced him, kissed him. But she never stopped watching him.

"Where's Rachel?" asked Gina.

"She should be here shortly," said Sam. "She's driving over from Lucy's. She spent the night there."

"She and Dad had another one of their religious discussions," said Wally.

"That will be enough, Wally," said Barbara.

"Well, come on over and say hello to Aaron," said Gina, gesturing toward the sofa, where he was struggling up onto his crutches. "Aaron, you remember my father, Sam Rossi."

The two men looked each other in the eye, muttered appropriate responses, and clenched each other's hand in firm, manly style. The introductions continued, to Barbara, to Wally, but her father never took his eyes off Aaron.

"Sorry to hear about your accident," said Sam, lingering near the sofa. "I could see right where you fell outside. The lights stop halfway around the back window."

Aaron gave Gina a silent, patient look. Criticism number one. "That's where the lights stop, all right," said Aaron. "Due to circumstances beyond our control."

Sam smiled. "Things do get out of control, don't they?"

Aaron gave Gina's father an appraising look. "Out of control every time you look the other way."

"Looking the other way," said Sam, "can be a big mistake."

The living room went silent.

The front door suddenly clattered open.

"Merry Christmas, everybody!" Rachel Rossi hurried in, red-cheeked, flecked with melting snowflakes. "Hope I'm not late."

She threw herself into her sister's arms.

"Not at all," said Gina, kissing her. She whispered in Rachel's ear. "Now, be good. Please."

117

"Hi, Mom," said Rachel. She gave Barbara the usual faint peck on the cheek. "Hi, Dad." Her greeting to her father was decidedly less casual, tense with defiance. "Uncle Tony!" she screamed, hugging him. "It's so great to see you!" Her greeting to Uncle Tony was much warmer and noisier than anything bestowed on either of her parents. They both noticed. She meant them to notice.

"Well, here we are," said Rachel, cheerfully ironic, as she hugged her grandparents. "Just one big, happy family."

6
Dinner Is Served

A taxi pulled up in front of the house, through streaming, swirling clouds of white.

The back door of the cab swung open impatiently before the driver could stomp through the snow to open it. The old woman who climbed out was overweight but spry, and determined to be around for a few more years. The snow did not impress her. She had seen worse. Snow was irritating and treacherous, nothing more. Aunt Jo was eighty-one years old, Orsola's kid sister. She had never married and had managed to endure a long, uneventful life. She was luxuriously bundled in a fur overcoat and had colored her hair silver blue.

Her unmistakable rapping at the door was chipper and aggressive, announcing that Aunt Jo had arrived.

"You didn't think I was afraid of a little snow, did you?" She thrust a fruitcake at Gina as she came through the door. "Well, the day I don't come to a family Christmas dinner, you'll know your Aunt Jo is dead." Her cheeks over-rouged, wearing too many jewels, she swept through the other family members like an aging movie star.

"You remember Aaron, don't you, Aunt Jo?"

"Of course, I do. I'm not so old that I'm losing my memory. Besides, I never forget a nice-looking young man."

Her mindless, good-humored chatter managed to provide a social lubricant to ease the jagged edges between family members. Ease, but not erase.

Slowly, in spite of her banter, everyone became thoroughly ill at ease. The conversation died. An awkward silence was strangling the living room by the time Gina stepped through the kitchen doorway. She unfastened the tie-strings of her apron behind her.

"Time to turn off the television and sit down at the table," she said. "Dinner is served."

Everyone rumbled into the dining room, shuffling and bumping toward their designated chairs. To sighs of appreciation on all sides, Rachel and Gloria carried in two long plates of antipasto, studded with Greek olives and artichoke hearts, fringed by slices of Swiss cheese and salami. They were placed at each end of the table. Aaron poured the wine.

"Grandpa," said Gina, "would you say grace?"

Lou reached out on either side of him, as all the Rossis awkwardly joined hands around the table.

"Bless this family, Lord," he said, "and this delicious food we're about to eat. Keep us all healthy, loving, and together." He nearly stopped and then impulsively added, "And bless my mother, Lord, bless Nana, who would have loved to be here with us this Christmas Eve. Amen."

With murmurs of anticipation, the Rossis spread their napkins in their laps. Platter after platter was brought out of the kitchen and passed around the table. A heaping bowl of steaming yellow polenta. Hot, slippery moustaccioli swimming in dark red sauce. Spicy sausages and meatballs and spareribs so tender the meat was crumbling off the bone.

But the strained warmth of the Rossi family was only surface deep. Conversation lurched and faltered. The only safety lay in eating. Everyone ate until they were stuffed.

*

Gina was passing the platter of meatballs down to Aunt Jo for one last serving when she noticed that her grandfather's cheeks were wet. She quickly pushed back her chair and hurried to his side.

"Grandpa, what is it?"

"Nothing, nothing," he said dismissively, wiping at his eyes as though they were scarcely worth the effort. "Absolutely nothing. It's just that — whoever could have dreamed that I would be sitting here again, here in this house, eating this food, the food that my mother used to—"

He cut off abruptly and rose to his feet.

"We need to let our food digest before we have dessert. I think it's time for some Christmas carols."

Everyone knew what that meant. Rachel and Gina gave excited cries. "Grandpa's going to play the accordion!"

Wally groaned. "Oh, boy, Christmas carols."

Lou heroically lugged his accordion out of its battered carrying case. It had traveled with him ever since his days in the Navy. Its ivory keys had been bleached yellow by the hot sun of the South Pacific. Securing the straps around his shoulders, he moved to the open archway into the living room, while all around him chairs were shuffled and turned around.

He jiggled the bellows, tried a few chords. Then he showed off with a march. He followed it with "I'm Dreaming of a White Christmas." Then came "Oh, Come All Ye Faithful." One by one, the family began hesitantly singing, generally on tune, momentarily forgetting themselves, almost happy.

Grandpa's accordion was just wheezing out the opening of "Deck the Halls" when the lights began to flicker.

Then the house went totally dark.

CHAPTER TWELVE

Dark Christmas

1
Faulty Wiring

"Okay, who leaned against the light switch?" said Barbara, peering into the darkness to spot the guilty party, her own two kids being the primary suspects.

No one apologized. No one giggled.

Gina felt her way along the wall. The light switch toggled back and forth, on and off

No lights.

"The power must be out," said Lou.

"It should come right back on," said Sam authoritatively. "Happens all the time during the winter. Little power outages. This snow doesn't help."

They sat awkwardly in the darkness, waiting. The lights didn't snap back on. They could hear the accordion groaning as Grandpa eased his arms out of the straps, the bellows wheezing as he lowered the instrument to the floor.

"How about the neighbors?" said Uncle Tony. "Maybe it's the whole block. Wally, can you see anything out there?"

Wally jumped up to look, moved too suddenly toward the window. He banged head-on into something. "Ouch!" He stumbled to the window and drew the curtain aside. "The people next door have lights." He continued staring out the window. "Boy, it sure is snowing hard."

"It must be the Christmas decorations," said Aaron. "We've obviously overloaded the circuit. Now, don't anybody move and get hurt. I'll go take care of the fuse box."

"Don't be silly, Aaron," objected Gina. "Not with your foot like that. A fuse box can't be that complicated."

"Nonsense." Aaron was already standing on his one good foot. "I'm not even taking my crutches. It's just a hop skip down the stairs. Stay right where you are. I don't want this wonderful evening to be spoiled in any way."

"Aaron, you get off that foot," said Sam, putting down his cup of coffee and pushing back his chair. "Let someone else take care of it." He considered rising, then looked across the table at his brother. "Let Tony do it. He's right there close to the basement door."

"Me?" said Uncle Tony. "You've got to be kidding. Find the fuse box in the dark? I don't know a thing about fuses."

"What's there to know?" said his brother. "You don't need an English degree to change a fuse. Don't be so help-less."

"I wouldn't exactly call myself helpless."

"You can't change a blown fuse?" said Sam. "Ah, the value of a liberal arts education!"

"At least I was interested in something besides money."

"Enough, you two," said Grandpa, rising. "I lived here for eighteen years. It won't take me a minute."

Sam tried to push his father back down in his chair. "You keep playing the accordion, Dad. I'll do it."

"You don't know where the fuse box is," said Lou. "I could find it blindfolded."

"Dad, I can figure it out," said Sam. "How hard can it be?"

"This is an old house," said Lou. "These aren't circuit-breakers, you know."

"Dad, I know how to change a fuse, believe me."

"Both of you, sit down," said Aaron decisively. "I'll take care of it. I'm the host." His tone of voice startled the Rossis and ended the discussion, leaving no room for alternatives. "Relax and stay right where you are. Nothing to worry about. Gina, where do we keep the candles?"

In answer, a match was struck. A flame leaped into existence, which moved toward the wick of a candle held up in front of Gina's smiling, triumphant face.

122

"Ta da," she said. "Let there be light."

Rachel and Wally clapped. Aunt Jo wasn't quite as enthusiastic. She was clearly flustered and quite unhappy.

"We'll need a lot more light than that," said Aunt Jo gloomily. "How upsetting! Electricity is so dangerous. Do you know how many people die every year from faulty electrical wiring?"

"How many, Aunt Jo?"

"You don't want to know."

"Well, you don't have to worry," said Gina to her great-aunt. "Aaron knows all about electricity."

"Now, don't exaggerate, Gina. It's just one of my little hobbies, Aunt Jo. Being self-sufficient. I like to be able to fix my own things."

"Electricity is one of his specialties," said Gina, enjoying an opportunity to brag about Aaron. "He's going to rewire the whole house for me." She did love him so. She wanted her family to see how special he was.

Aaron was blushing. "Sooner or later," he amended. "Hopefully I won't have to rewire the whole house tonight. I'll be right back up." He awkwardly pushed in his dinner chair and hobbled just far enough into the dark kitchen to slide open a drawer. He rummaged blindly through the contents.

"Be careful on those stairs!" called Gina after him.

He turned back toward her, and a blinding beam of light suddenly struck her between the eyes. "Don't worry about me," said Aaron. "I've got my trusty flashlight."

2
Descent

The wobbling circle of light guided him down the steep basement staircase. Stair by stair, he made his way, favoring the foot in the splint, supporting his weight on the other foot and the handrail, until he could feel the solid, cement floor underneath him.

The descent took a little more energy than he expected. He caught his breath, orienting himself.

The basement seemed much bigger in the dark. He tried to remember where he had piled boxes and crates. The flashlight beam poked out a path for him through the darkness, wavering and jiggling toward the cantina.

The fuse box was just beyond the old-fashioned washtub, inside the small, poorly-designed wine cellar. It was tucked behind the two barrels, like an ancient medicine cabinet with a cast-iron door. The words "American Electric" across the front radiated bold, confident thunderbolts.

Halfway there, a sound stopped him in his tracks. At first he thought it was a creaking stair. He listened.

Someone was crying.

Not pigeons. That much he was sure of. It was a child in tears. He tilted his head forward, straining his ears, trying to detect where it was coming from. His flashlight beam swept the basement. The sound seemed to originate outside. Out in that cold, swirling whiteness.

The round, bright circle from his flashlight picked out his old plastic rain jacket hanging from its nail. His arms were poking through the sleeves, his hands shoving aside the bolt, before he realized he was opening the basement door.

A white blast slammed into him, surged into the basement, flapping out his rain jacket in crackling confusion.

He left the basement door open. Like a one-legged man, he hopped a few steps into the deep, crunching white shell that had covered the world. He hobbled awkwardly, trying to keep the exposed stocking of his splinted foot from getting too soaked with snow. The cries seemed to be coming from the direction of the vegetable garden. He pushed away from the corner of the house, blindly reaching out. But where exactly was the garden in all that white upheaval?

Where, for that matter, was the house?

What was happening? Was this what they called a mild Northwest winter? Suddenly he realized the sheer deadly potential of getting lost in that blinding turbulence. He could see nothing but snow, in every direction. He took a step backward, then another, backing the way he'd come, retreating into his own footprints. He had to tug at the basement door to make it close against the storm.

It was suddenly very quiet.

The thick, wool stocking protecting his splinted foot was soaked. Bracing himself against the wall, balancing on one leg, he peeled the wet sock off his foot, drying his icy, wet toes on the other pantleg. The cement floor was freezing cold underfoot. He listened. Nothing. No child out in the snow. Could he have been imagining things?

Well, he wasn't imagining Gina's unhappy family sitting upstairs in the dark, waiting for him.

Without taking off the rain jacket, he headed straight for the fuse box. It would only take a minute. In the stillness of the basement, Aaron unexpectedly heard it again. A weak, little sob. Then it all became clear to him. He had been looking in the wrong place. It wasn't outside at all.

The sob had come from inside the cantina.

3
Disappearing Act

Did Wally blow out the candle?

Or was it a nervous sigh, someone's sudden movement, a gust of air?

"Not again!" groaned Aunt Jo.

"Just let me find the matches," said Gina, groping about the coffee table. "I thought I put them right over here."

There was something volatile and tense about the suddenly renewed darkness. Apparently it went to Wally's head. His sense of humor was definitely teenage level.

"Hey, who's doing that?" said Wally, deadly serious, squirming uncomfortably in his chair. "Oh. Someone's touching me. Stop that. Oh. Oh—"

Rachel started giggling nervously.

"That'll be enough, Wally," said his father. "If you can't make adult conversation, be quiet."

"I was just trying to be funny," said Wally.

"Well, you failed," snapped his father.

A crash in the dark.

"What happened?"

"I think that was Wally's chair."

"Wally? Wally?"

Suddenly the lights of the chandelier above the dining-room table flickered on uncertainly. So did the living-room lamps, the Christmas tree lights. With cries of relief and approval, everyone clapped and cheered.

But not for long. The return of illumination revealed that one of the dining-room chairs, reversed to face Grandpa's accordion performance, now lay overturned on the floor.

"Where's Wally?" said Barbara anxiously. She rose. 'That boy—!" She knew she was being maternal, but she couldn't help it. The old house gave her the creeps. "Sam, he was just being a silly, nervous kid. You shouldn't talk to him like that."

"I'll find him," said Sam. He could read her mind and he knew she was right. He tried to be a good father, but a son like Wally tested his limits severely.

He rose from the table.

"No," said Barbara. "Now is not the time to go find him, Sam. Not until you calm down."

"Who knows what trouble he could get into in an old house like this?" said Sam. "You know what he's like when he's upset. The things he does sometimes aren't very smart. I want to know where my son is."

"Leave him alone, Sam." Her tone was respectful but unwavering. "Calm down first."

"Speaking of knowing where people are," said Gina. She left her sentence unfinished. She glanced anxiously over her shoulder, toward the stairs leading down to the basement. "Aaron seems to be taking an awfully long time at the fuse box."

The lights went out again.

Everyone groaned.

4
Trapped

Gina found the matches. The candle leaped back into life.

Their faces, lit by candlelight, were not happy. Consensus opinion of Aaron's electrical skills had plunged. No one felt like singing any more Christmas carols. Grandpa loaded his accordion back into its case. Outside the wind was howling. A string of Christmas lights was tearing loose from the house across the street.

"Take a look at your neighbor's house," pointed out Aunt Jo. "Nothing wrong with their lights."

"Aaron will have ours working any minute," said Gina. "Absolutely nothing to fret about, Aunt Jo." She knew better than to go downstairs and offer to help him. Household repairs with Aaron were a masculinity issue. He could be very sensitive.

Sam had gone to the coat closet and was pulling on his blue ski parka. "I'm just going outside to check the van." He opened the front door. "Don't want to get ourselves snowed in."

A sudden howling coldness swept through the house, flapping curtains, blowing over Christmas cards, chilling everyone it touched with a mean and icy sting.

"Close the door!" wailed Barbara, Gloria, and Aunt Jo, all at the same time.

The living room door slammed. A few moments later the engine began revving stubbornly in the driveway.

Grandma and Grandpa were huddled together by the living room window, nervously peering out through the lace curtains at the condition of the streets. Neither Lou nor Gloria trusted their eyesight in the dark. Their reflexes weren't as quick as they used to be. Unusual circumstances, unpredictable conditions, frightened them. The snow was coming down harder.

The lights abruptly brightened, then blazed white-hot, then dimmed and flickered half-heartedly.

127

"There, now that's better!" sighed Gina. "At least we're halfway back to normal." Her sentiments were echoed all around the living-room.

"Lights shouldn't act like that," grumbled Aunt Jo.

"It's some kind of power spike," said Sam.

They waited, watching the lights, scarcely daring to breathe. The lights stayed on.

Gina blew out the candle in front of her. "We'd better save the candles for when we need them."

"We should probably get going before things get worse," said Grandma uneasily.

"But we haven't opened the presents yet," objected Rachel.

"Those streets are going to be slippery," said Grandpa. "And the later it gets, the more ice—"

"Well, then, let's open the presents right now," said Barbara. If anything would bring Wally back, it was opening presents. "While we still have some light to see them by." She rose to her feet and headed toward the twinkling branches of the tree. "Who's going to help me sort them into piles?"

"You go ahead," said Grandma. "But we really do need to get going."

"You and Grandma aren't going anywhere," said Gina decisively. "This is no weather to be driving in. There's plenty of room right here. You can spend the night."

"Oh, no, we couldn't," said Grandma.

"Listen," said Gina, "it would take me about two minutes to get sheets and blankets on one of the beds upstairs."

"We wouldn't want to put you to all that trouble."

"No trouble at all. I'd be delighted."

"Now, now," said Grandma. "I'm sure Grandpa can—"

But Grandpa wasn't as sure as she was. Lou was looking out the window and shook his head. He put his arm around his wife. "Gina's right, hon. We better make ourselves comfortable. We're going to be here for a while."

The door blew open to admit Sam's snow-whitened blue ski parka along with a few swirling, insistent snowflakes. The door promptly whooshed shut.

"Doesn't look like we'll be going anywhere," said Sam. His cheeks were flushed bright pink with the cold. "That snow is coming down hard. Can't see a thing out there." He turned to Barbara. "Honey, I can't seem to find the car phone."

"It should be right where it always is," said Barbara. "I even re-charged it, just to be extra safe—" She gasped. "Oh, Sam, I must have left it in the kitchen re-charging!"

"Oh-oh," said Rachel. "Looks like someone will have to survive without his cellular phone."

"Don't be a smartmouth, young lady," said Barbara.

"Just an observation," said Rachel.

"Well, I'm happy to have you all stay," said Gina. "Every one of you. There's plenty of room. It will be like a big family slumber party on Christmas Eve."

"It sounds unwise, unpractical, and uncomfortable," said Aunt Jo. "As far as I'm concerned, it's out of the question."

"Oh, now Aunt Jo," said Rachel, "be a good sport. I think we're all going to have lots of fun here, pretending like we're not trapped."

The lights flickered, wavered, but managed to stay on. The winking of the lights reminded Gina painfully of who was missing.

"Make yourselves at home," she said. She could no longer restrain her mounting anxiety. "If you'll excuse me, I've got to find out what's keeping Aaron so long. If he's gotten involved in one of his home repairs, we may never see him again."

5
Gone

"Aaron?"

No answer.

"Aaron, you're being rude. Whatever it is, it can wait."

His silence only increased her uneasiness. No sign of him in the weakly-lit basement. The cantina door was open.

She descended the rest of the way down the stairs, crossed the basement, and mounted the three stairs to the cantina. The light wasn't on inside.

"Aaron?"

She became tense with a sudden, illogical dread. She forced herself to crouch down and enter. She pulled the light cord, ready to rush to his aid.

The cantina was empty. Just a small, silent room full of mousetraps, baited and waiting.

"Aaron?"

The word echoed hollowly in the cramped little cellar. There were the wine barrels and the fuse box and the empty planks of shelving. But no Aaron. She turned around in the cantina doorway, heart pounding in confusion.

She made her way across the basement, through a maze of boxes and crates to the other side. The door leading out to the vegetable garden was closed but no longer bolted. And something was missing. The nail by the door was bare. His rain jacket was gone. Impulsively, she turned the latch, seized the doorknob, and tugged the old door open.

A shrieking gale of coldness at once engulfed her, howling, stinging—

"Aaron!" she shouted. Snowflakes sliced at her eyes, rushed at her face, driving her back into the basement, like no snow she had ever known. The wind shoved the word right back down her throat.

She slammed the door shut.

But it had been open long enough for her to see the footprints starting out into the blanket of snow, footprints that disappeared at the corner of the house. With just an old rain jacket, with his foot in a splint, hobbling without his crutches, Aaron had left the house through the basement door, without a word to anyone.

But why?

Could he really be that upset with her family? Surely he wasn't abandoning her! But, if not, then where could he have gone? He had to be there somewhere. This was the real world. People didn't vanish into the snow. Gina walked slowly back and forth across the dark basement, hugging herself to keep from shaking, fighting off shuddering attacks of disbelief.

What should she do? *Could* she do?

She became so frightened, facing the impossible fact of Aaron's disappearance, that she decided one thing for sure. Under no circumstances would she terrify the others with her discovery. They didn't have to know about the vanishing of their host. It was better not to know.

6
Remedy

Aunt Jo didn't miss a thing. Her sharp, old eyes were watching Gina the moment she stepped back into the living room.

"And did you find your wandering boyfriend?"

Gina smiled grimly. It was a smile of sheer will-power, an impenetrable wall against the intrusive curiosity of her great-aunt. "Looks like he's gone down to the Seven-Eleven."

"No! In this weather?"

"Before it gets any worse. It's just a block down the street."

"On Christmas Eve?"

"They never close. He must have needed to buy a box of fuses. The ones we've got seem to be going bad. That must be the problem." She hoped.

Aunt Jo didn't buy it for a minute. "Gina, I may be an old woman but I'm not stupid. Are you trying to tell me your boyfriend just walked to the store in this snowstorm? With his foot in a splint? Without his crutches?"

She had to admit, it didn't sound very likely. She didn't even attempt to defend her theory. "You don't have to worry about Aaron, Aunt Jo. He's a big boy."

"Big boys are the worst."

"Excuse me," said Rachel to her sister, interrupting. "Do you have a hairbrush I can use?"

"Sure, sis," said Gina. "There's one in the bathroom."

Grateful for the interruption, Gina took her sister's hand and led her out of the dining room, through the living room, and down the hall.

"Are you okay?" whispered Rachel urgently, watching her sister's troubled face. "That old bag doesn't know when to quit."

"I'm okay," said Gina. "Thanks."

Rachel wasn't convinced. "Did you and Aaron have a fight? Gina, what is it? Tell me."

Gina's voice cracked. "I can't talk about it right now."

She left Rachel in the bathroom. She heard her sister lock the door behind her. Instead of returning to her guests, Gina hurried the rest of the way down the hall and crossed the master bedroom to the window. He had to be somewhere near! There had to be some trace, some clue. Below, through the frosty glass, she could see Aaron's footprints, starting out from the basement door. They came to an abrupt halt in the middle of uninterrupted whiteness. Without explanation, without a clue.

With a whimper of frustration, Gina returned to the others gathered in the living room. She tried not to think about him. He could take care of himself. He'd have some perfectly good reason for his strange behavior. She immersed herself in comforting her flustered parents and irritated aunt.

"Believe me, we'll all look back on this and laugh," said Gina confidently. "Come on, let me show you those rooms upstairs."

Her parents were willing, attempting to gracefully adapt to an awkward situation. Her great-aunt refused to budge.

"Absolutely not," said Aunt Jo. "I'm not spending the night here and that's final. I will simply call a cab, just like I always do. I know the number by heart. It's their job to drive, regardless of the weather. I'm sure a professional taxi driver can handle a little snow."

She picked up the phone and punched in the number. She waited impatiently, tapping her foot. The expression of resolution on her face slowly underwent a change. "There's something wrong with your phone."

"Nonsense," said Gina, taking the receiver away from her. "I'm sure it's fine." It wasn't fine. Gina pushed the disconnect several times. No dial tone. "It must be the snow. It'll be working again in no time. But you'd be foolish to try to leave, Aunt Jo. It's much safer right here."

"I'm never foolish," said Aunt Jo, "and this old house of my sister's does not strike me as particularly safe." The fear of interrupting her habits, of not returning to the predictable routines of her own home, of spending the night in an unfamiliar bed, made Aunt Jo even grouchier than usual.

"Now, it's not going to be that bad," said Gina optimistically, trying to bolster everyone's spirits. "I'm sure you'll all be perfectly comfy."

"No, we won't," objected Aunt Jo. "I'm uncomfortable just thinking about it. This is the worst Christmas of my entire life."

"Aunt Jo, I'm so sorry," said Gina, genuinely horrified to be responsible for such unpleasantness. Her glance wandered desperately about the living room and through the archway into the dining room. It lingered there on the polished wood of the old liquor cabinet. "But I may have a remedy for you."

"They don't write the prescription," grumbled Aunt Jo, as Gina strode past her, around the dining table, and opened the cabinet door. When Aunt Jo noticed that Gina was pouring something, she became more attentive.

"It's time for an after-dinner drink," said Gina. She handed Aunt Jo a glass goblet of red wine. She continued pouring and passing around sloshing goblets to the others. "I want you all to drink a toast of Christmas cheer with me. We can use some cheer, don't you think?"

A general grumbled assent.

"May we love one another, be tolerant of one another, and remember that we are a family." She raised her wine glass. "To being a family."

"A family," echoed everyone else, following the words with the appropriate activity.

Gina tipped her head back to drink. The goblet froze at her lips. What was she thinking? Alcohol for a pregnant woman? She returned her wine to the table untouched. When she looked up, she found all the eyes of her family watching her. Everyone had silently noticed her not drinking. Everyone knew why.

Everyone except Aunt Jo, who was too busy coughing down half the contents of her goblet. "My, that's strong." More coughing. Gloria slapped her helpfully on the back. "I'm not used to it. But under the circumstances—" She took another cautious swallow, and another. "It does warm up these old bones. Thank you, my dear, this is exactly what was needed. Much better. Well, whoever would have thought that I'd be spending the night at my sister's house? Orsola never invited me over while she was alive. She's making up for lost time."

She chuckled and examined the bottom of her empty goblet. "I don't suppose I could have just a tiny drop more?"

7
Family Secrets

"It wasn't easy being Orsola's sister," said Aunt Jo. "Let me tell you, Orsola didn't share the stage. Not with anyone." She sipped at her refill. "This really does help the nerves. I never touch it, usually. Orsola did. She liked her sip, that girl. She could be a wild one."

Uncle Tony laughed. "Come on, Aunt Jo. I'd hardly call Nana wild. Her idea of wild would be hunting for wild dandelions to make into a salad."

Aunt Jo snorted. "It's time you all stopped talking about your sweet Nana like she was some kind of saint."

"Well, she practically was—" began Tony.

His brother cut him off. "Hardly," said Sam. "I agree with Aunt Jo. Nana was no saint, and that's for sure."

"Now, what's that supposed to mean?" said Gina, trying not to let her father upset her, to preserve her nervous smile.

"I'll tell you about your dear Nana," said Sam impulsively. "She made my childhood miserable."

"What are you talking about?" interrupted Lou, shocked to hear his mother referred to so disrespectfully by his own son.

"I was never good enough for Nana," said Sam. "You know that as well as I do, Dad. No matter how great my grades were, no matter how many times I lettered in sports, no matter how many honors I got, I just wasn't as good as Tony. Tony had done it all first and done it better. Tony could do no wrong. As for little Sammy, well, he was cute but he hardly mattered. All that mattered was Tony."

"Why, that's ridiculous!" exclaimed Uncle Tony, a little louder than he intended. "Nana loved you just as much as—"

"Hogwash," said Sam. "Nothing I did mattered. Everything you touched was gold. I just wasn't good enough for Nana."

"Orsola had her dark side," agreed Aunt Jo, extending her empty glass toward the nearly depleted bottle. "That girl could be a devil. Selfish, unfair, heartless! Oh, but when she and Niccolo got together — she liked the boys, I can tell you." She laughed in a very knowing manner.

"Aunt Jo, do you really think this is appropriate?" Lou tried to interrupt her. She was enjoying herself too much to heed his warning.

"Orsola used to go with Niccolo back into the old garage," said Aunt Jo. "I watched her once. I hid in the garage before they got there. You should have seen them kiss!"

Lou was not amused. "Aunt Jo, you've had enough."

"She had a crazy streak, Orsola did. She could be stubborn as hell. She could get favors out of anyone. Let me tell you, if my sister wanted something, the Pope himself couldn't refuse her."

"Aunt Jo, listen to yourself. You're exaggerating."

"Am I? She had a guilty conscience, if you ask me. Got her way once too often. I wouldn't be surprised if my dear sister took a few secrets to the grave. It's no wonder she did what she did. I would have ended it, too."

At first Aunt Jo didn't seem to notice the effect of her words. The frozen expressions. The abrupt silence.

"Ended it?" repeated Gina, breaking the shocked still-ness with a tardy echo.

Aunt Jo turned in surprise toward Lou. "Your Grandpa never told you? You've got to be kidding me. Now, Lou, that's ridiculous. It's nothing to hide. It's just a part of life."

"A part I'd like to forget," said Lou. "A part I see no reason to rub in the faces of those I love."

"What do you mean, ended it?" repeated Gina.

"I thought you knew," said Aunt Jo. "Lou, you ought to be ashamed. Keeping secrets from your family. Well, are you going to tell them, or shall I?"

"It's part of the past, Aunt Jo," objected Lou. "Leave it in the past."

"You don't think your granddaughter deserves to know what happened in her own house?"

"What is it, Grandpa?" said Gina. "Something happened here that I don't know about?"

Lou sighed. "Something you would have been happier not knowing about."

"Tell me," said Gina.

"Looks like I have to, since your Aunt Jo can't leave it alone." He took a deep breath. "The only way to explain is to admit that I lied to you." Another long, slow breath. "I never put Nana in a nursing home."

"What?" said Gloria. His own wife looked at him in sheer confusion. "Of course you did, Lou. Are you losing your mind? Nana died the day after you put her there. Didn't she?"

"No," said Lou sadly. "That's just what I told you. The only lie in all the years we've been married, but I didn't want you to know. Any of you. I didn't want you to think of her that way. It was bad enough her sister found out."

"But why?" said Gloria. "Lou, why?" The question seemed to catch in her throat. Her husband had lied to her. It was unthinkable.

"Why should you have to know something like that?" said Lou. "You should remember Nana the way she was, not—" His voice cracked. He hardened it. "She was a poor, unhappy old woman, and when the day came for her to leave her house, she was desperate, terrified, out of her mind. She didn't want to go on living. She—"

"Nana died here?" said Gina. The words barely made it out of her mouth.

"Yes," said Lou. "She refused to leave. She chose to die here, instead." He turned to regard his aunt with quiet contempt. "Satisfied, Aunt Jo? Now are you happy?"

8
Dead Line

"Secrets!" Aunt Jo drained what was left of her wine and set the empty goblet down with a clumsy rattle. "You should know better than that, Lou. Trying to keep secrets from your own flesh and blood!" She shifted uncomfortably. "Secrets are the worst things that can happen to a family." She shifted again. "I'm afraid all this wine is catching up with me." She glanced toward the hallway. "Is Rachel still in the bathroom?"

"Of course," said Sam. "It's been less than an hour. She's just getting started." He cupped his hands around his mouth. "Rachel," he yelled, "you can't tie up the bathroom all night."

"I'm hurrying," shouted Rachel from the bathroom.

Her words were not encouraging.

"There's a bathroom upstairs," suggested Lou, remembering his childhood, remembering how many times he had raced up there to use it. "If you don't mind the stairs."

"I can still manage stairs just fine, thank you," snapped his aunt. "I'm not that old yet, Lou. Just tell me where to find it. And make it quick."

"Turn to your left at the top of the stairs. Then go all the way to the end of the hall."

"I'll be right back." She was already on her way out of the living room, scuttling in a reasonably straight line toward the staircase door, which she flung open.

"Where's the light?" she complained.

"Right next to the door. You can feel it on the wall."

She clearly found it, for her heavy footfalls began shaking the house as she trudged, stair by stair, up to the second floor, lowering her full weight onto every stair. After a worrisome pause while she caught her breath, her footsteps thudded down the hall. A distant door, presumably leading into the upstairs bathroom, slammed.

Relieved, the family began to talk about other things, to resume faltering conversations.

A scream cut through the house.

Sam and Gina were the first ones up the stairs. They heard her body falling over before they got to the bathroom. Sam shoved open the door. She was crumpled on the floor, half-curled around the toilet. Her face was a rigid mask of fear. Sam dropped to her side, taking her wrist to feel for a pulse.

"Call the doctor," he yelled over his shoulder to his daughter. Gina immediately rushed for the telephone down the hall. She anxiously punched in 9-1-1.

Nothing.

She slammed down the receiver in frustration. She stood trembling over the telephone, gripping it as though she dared not let go. The solid foundations of her world were crumbling. Aaron had descended into the basement and vanished. She had discovered that Nana died in the house. And now Aunt Jo had been terrified out of her senses. By what?

"The line is dead," she called to her father.

Sam swore under his breath. "Maybe your neighbors' phone is working," he said. "I'll go next door and see if they'll let me make a call."

He didn't wait for a reply. Sam Rossi went down the stairs two at a time, and was shoving his arms into his blue ski parka as he strode toward the door.

"Sam, be careful!" called Barbara.

The door slammed behind him.

CHAPTER THIRTEEN

The Love That Wasn't There

1
In Aunt Jo's Room

Other than an occasional sputtering, the lights had managed to stay on.

Gina didn't need much light. Just enough to slide the corners of the fitted sheet around the ends of the mattress, enough to flap out a sheet and a comforter and a pillowcase, to make an emergency bed for her aunt.

Nana had died here. That thought came back to her, again and again. She had chosen to die rather than leave her house.

How she longed to have Aaron's arms around her now. She tried not to think about Aaron. If she let herself think about him, she'd crack. How could he possibly be gone this long? She had peered out of every window, searching for any clue. She forced herself to forget those footprints disappearing into the snow. She forced herself to think about the bed in front of her, about tucking in the blankets, about plumping the pillows.

She could hear heavy footsteps approaching. A floppy, boneless Aunt Jo appeared in the doorway, propped up on one side by Grandpa, on the other side by Uncle Tony. They guided her into the bedroom, lowered her onto the bed.

She scarcely seemed to know where she was. Gina unbuttoned her collar and tried to make her comfortable. Aunt Jo's heart was thudding wildly. The family hovered around the bedside and in the doorway. Suddenly the snowfall seemed the least of their problems. They might be sharing a house with death that Christmas.

Gina leaned over her, concerned, attentive.

"Aunt Jo, what happened?"

The older woman seemed willing to tell her, if only her mouth and lips would obey. Meaningless sounds were all she could produce.

"Don't worry, Aunt Jo," she said. "Dad's gone to phone for the doctor. We'll get someone here to take care of you."

She heard the front door slam, then her father's footsteps mounting the stairs. His cheeks were flushed red, his parka edged with snow.

"No one's home," he said. "I tried to get to the neighbors across the street. The snow is coming down so hard you can't see where you're going." He hated admitting defeat.

His words caused Gina a shiver of pure terror. "I've never heard of it snowing like this in Seattle," she said. "I don't suppose you happened to see any sign of Aaron?"

"Couldn't see much of anything." He turned toward the bed. "How is she?"

"She's doing fine," said Gloria. "No need for a doctor. She's just very scared." She wasn't the only one. All the faces around Aunt Jo's bed were scared. In a lower voice, Gloria added, "And she's a little bit drunk. She'll feel better after a rest."

Gina fought down her fears. Aaron would be all right. She looked across the bed into the wide and frightened eyes of her younger sister. Rachel's lower lip was trembling.

"What do you think happened to her?" said Rachel.

"She had too much to drink, that's all."

"But then, why did she scream?"

Lou was trying very hard not to ask himself that same question. "You never know, Rachel. Old ladies do some pretty crazy things sometimes."

"Something scared her," said Rachel. She was remembering her own experience trapped on the back porch. "This house is scary."

"Now, now," said Lou. "It's just an old house. Old houses creak and groan, but that's all there is to it."

"No, Grandpa, she's right," said Gina. "Sometimes you hear things in this house. You see things. Not just Rachel. It's happened to me, too. And to Aaron, and Uncle Tony. And now that I know Nana died here — well, you can't help but think that in some way, maybe, Nana could be — you know, still here."

"I don't believe I heard that," said Sam. "Four years of college and you believe in ghosts."

"She may be closer to the truth than you think," said Uncle Tony. "There's something seriously wrong in this house.'

"Now, don't start filling my kids with your crazy—"

"It's almost like Nana never left," persisted Uncle Tony.

"You're talking complete nonsense," said Gloria to her son. "You know perfectly well—"

Aunt Jo moaned faintly, interrupting them. She had something she urgently wanted to say. She tried very hard to say it. She managed to blow a thin saliva bubble.

"Please don't die, Aunt Jo," said Rachel.

"She isn't going to die," said Grandma. "It takes more than wine to kill someone as tough as Aunt Jo."

Responding to her name, the old woman tried again to speak. Her lips opened and shut, like a fish out of water. All she wanted to say was one word. She finally managed to say it.

"Orsola."

*

Rachel turned away from the bed. She had never been so scared in her life. She could feel her father standing beside her. He had shrugged out of his wet parka and was holding his wet shoes, bleakly watching the snowfall through the window.

"It hasn't stopped all day," she said.

"Doesn't look like it's going to."

"You can't see a thing out there." She peered out the window, trying to distract herself. All she could see was whirling white and darkness, thrown together, blurred into one. "It's like somebody erased everything." She nervously reached out for her father's hand, something she hadn't done for several years. "It's like nothing's out there anymore."

"It's all still there," said Sam. "You may not be able to see it, but the world never goes away."

"Is Aunt Jo going to be all right?"

"I don't know," said her father. "I hope so, but you never know. You never know about anybody."

For a brief moment, Sam and his daughter, Rachel, stood together in an intimate closeness to which they had both become strangers. It didn't last.

"If you still remember how to pray," he said, "maybe you ought to say a few prayers for your aunt."

Rachel jerked her hand away. "As if what she really needs is a little Catholic mumbo-jumbo."

"Listen, young lady, I'm warning you—" Sam was suddenly very close to losing his temper.

"If you're so keen on prayers, say them yourself!" cried Rachel. "I just hope they do you some good, because they won't be doing much good for her."

She stormed out of the room.

2
No Place to Hide

No sketchbook!

Wally had forgotten it downstairs in the haste of his departure. He would have to do without it. Besides, there wasn't enough light to do much drawing. He had his stash, at least, wrapped in aluminum foil and secreted away in the pocket of his jeans. That would be enough. A couple puffs would calm him down nicely. He had wanted those puffs badly enough to fumble and bump his way through the scary darkness of Gina's house to make his getaway.

The electrical outage had been the perfect opportunity.

He had fled in reckless haste, expecting the lights of the house to come back on at any moment. He found his way up the stairs to the second floor. After that he wasn't sure exactly which direction he went. As his eyes became adjusted to the darkness, patches of windowlight guided him from doorway to doorway.

He found his way through a room at the end of the hall into a large closet. He was just making himself comfortable at the far end of it when he noticed a small door. He bumped the door and it swung open, into a very narrow staircase, with a tiny window near the top providing just enough light to see.

The perfect place to get mellow.

Wally scrambled up five stairs and made himself comfortable, with his back against the wall. The hand-rolled joint in his pocket was crunched and bent, but still smokable. His lighter flared.

He was so busy puffing that he didn't notice the cloud of smoke he was creating in the tight little staircase. He didn't notice much of anything, since the marijuana, combined with all the food he'd just eaten, was making him very sleepy.

*

He jolted upright, eyes wide, the scream still ringing in his ears. Who had screamed?

Wally was afraid to budge. He could hear footsteps running up the staircase. He could hear Gina and his Dad shouting in the other hall. What had happened? Then more footsteps as other members of his family rushed upstairs. Wally clenched his teeth. He wanted to be left alone. He did not want to be found and humiliated.

He was too stoned to hide his feelings. He could feel tears spilling hotly down his cheeks.

*

He didn't remember falling back asleep.

Thong—

He blinked open his eyes. At first he assumed he had caused the sound himself. It seemed to come from very

143

near. He must have leaned on a bad board, or bumped some-thing.

Thong—

He flinched. What was that? It seemed to come from inside the walls, as though the walls were hollow. Some-thing was wrong with that sound. It had too much of an echo. It seemed slightly warped, distorted. Or was that just because he was stoned?

Wally found himself starting to get scared.

Thong—

It wasn't his imagination. Something was hitting against the wall. Suddenly Wally found himself very much regretting that he was high. He had no way to assess what he was hearing. How much of that sound was real? How much was being amplified, exaggerated, by the marijuana? The old house was spooky enough without hearing sounds he couldn't explain. Where was it coming from? How close was it? Was he in danger?

And then all at once he knew.

It was his pesty sister, Rachel, teasing him as usual, trying to scare him with that irritating noise, bothering him when all he wanted was to be left alone.

He was alone no longer. Someone was standing at the foot of the stairs right now, looking up at him.

It was probably her.

3
"Wally, Is That You?"

Rachel hurried down the hall. Her Dad could drive her crazy! Fortunately, it was a big house. As far as she was concerned, the only compelling activity at the moment was getting as far as humanly possible away from her father.

The room at the end of the hall had a door on the far side. It opened into another room Rachel didn't remember. Maybe it wasn't really a room. It was too small.

Maybe it was a huge closet.

She heard a muffled sob. It seemed to come from nearby. Then she saw, at the rear of the closet, a tiny door.

"Wally, is that you?"

No response.

She stepped cautiously closer. All of her anxieties about Nana's house rushed to the surface. She reached out and touched the cold doorknob.

The door swung inward.

The smell practically knocked her over. The narrow passageway reeked of marijuana smoke. She pushed the door open wider, and stepped inside. A cramped, narrow staircase led upward, squeezed between two tight walls. She could detect a shadow slouched halfway up the stairs.

"Are you out of your mind?" said Rachel. "Do you want Dad to murder you?"

"What do you want?"

"I just wanted to make sure my little brother wasn't getting too freaked out."

"Well, are you satisfied?" said Wally, with a sulky defiance. "Was I supposed to feel better after your spooky noises? Close the door and leave me alone."

"Spooky noises?" She quickly closed the door, but only after she first stepped inside, shutting the door behind her to keep the smell from spreading. She could make out enough of her brother's face to see that his cheeks were streaked with tears.

"You okay?"

"I'm always okay." Wally swiped at his runny nose with the back of his wrist. "What's it to you?"

"Just checking," said Rachel, sitting down beside him. She made herself as comfortable as possible, appreciating the privacy of the spot. "So this is where you've been hiding?"

"I'm not hiding," said Wally. He could no longer restrain his curiosity. "So, what happened out there? All the shouting and running around."

"Oh, Aunt Jo had a few too many," said Rachel. "She fainted and everybody freaked out. She's in bed now, sleeping it off. She can be a real pain."

145

"How's Dad?" asked Wally. "Is he out for my blood?"

"You can't let Dad get to you."

"That's easy for you to say," said Wally. "You're not his son. My whole purpose in life is to disappoint that man."

"What's that supposed to mean?"

"Figure it out," said Wally. "First he has a daughter, and then he has another daughter, but finally he gets a boy, his Sammy Junior, his wish come true. But there's a problem. His son doesn't want to be a jock like Dad. Both his daughters want to be jocks—"

Rachel punched him in the shoulder.

"—but his son just wants to draw cartoons, and that is not Big Sam's idea of what a son should be. I'm a failure as a son, a Disappointment with a capital D."

"Come on, buck up!" She punched him again. "Compared to Dad, most people are failures. I mean, you've got to look at Dad realistically. He isn't just your basic overachiever. He's way, way beyond that. Just think how Uncle Tony must feel. I mean, he's his brother and Uncle Tony's like a total failure."

Both of them realized at the same time that someone was watching them.

Something moved in the shadows pooling at the foot of the staircase. Into the doorway stepped Uncle Tony, his shoulders filling the cramped space. He gave a couple of exploratory sniffs.

"Well, well, well." He sniffed again. "Someone's having a party and didn't invite me."

4
What Grandma Saw

Gloria Rossi knew only too well, as grandmother of her family, that if she wanted something done right, she had to do it herself. She'd had quite enough of this nonsense. Children didn't just disappear in a house. It was simply a matter of finding them and making them behave. She had

146

worried about Wally long enough. And now Rachel! It was time to take the bull by the horns.

She had been sitting by Aunt Jo's bedside, but Aunt Jo wouldn't be going anywhere. There were plenty of others to attend to the needs of a half-soused old woman. Uneasy about the safety of her grandchildren, Gloria couldn't sit still any longer.

Her husband knew her too well. "Where do you think you're going?" said Lou.

"Those two kids have no reason to be running all over this house, making trouble," she said. "They've got to learn to behave." With that, she strode out the door and halfway down the west hall.

"Wally! Rachel! You kids, answer me!"

Nothing.

Scowling, Gloria strode back the way she'd come, circled around the descending staircase, and started down the other hallway. "You kids come out this minute."

Nothing.

Her grandchildren's failure to reply unnerved her. They should have answered immediately. They respected and loved their grandmother. They never failed to obey her.

She stared down the dark, silent hallway. Not a rustle. But then she couldn't hear much of anything. Not so much as a murmur from all the voices in Aunt Jo's room, at the end of the other hall. Something was wrong with the acoustics in that house!

Without a moment more of hesitation, she headed toward the nearest guest room. Her footsteps crunched loudly across the floorboards. She poked her head through the doorway.

"Kids? You answer me, this minute!"

She vaguely remembered most of the rooms on the west hall, back where Aunt Jo was snoring, but during Nana's time the east hall had been used mostly for storage. Gloria stopped.

This was the east hall, wasn't it?

She recognized the second room she came to, and the third room. She did not remember the door at the end of the upstairs hallway. Nor the small room she found on the other side. Her memory was no longer what it used to be. Another turn, and Gloria found herself uncertain which direction she had just come from.

She returned to the end of the hall, but when she opened the door to leave, she found herself facing a closet. She closed the closet door in confusion and retraced her steps. Her forehead was beaded with sweat.

"Wally? Rachel?"

She had an anxious feeling in the pit of her stomach. Enough was enough. It was none of her business. Gloria was ready to stop interfering and return to her place among the others.

Except for one problem. Gloria was lost.

But how could someone get lost in a house? "Is it Alzheimer's?" she thought in panic. "Is it finally happening to me, too?"

At the far end of the hall she found another bedroom, one she had never seen before. She stopped in bewilderment. She felt dizzy. And she was starting to get cold. There was an icy draft coming from somewhere. Then her heart began to pound.

Someone, half-hidden in shadows, was watching her from the other end of the hall.

"Who is that?"

Whoever it was didn't budge.

"I see you there," she said sternly. "Wally? Rachel? You kids get over here right now."

A blurry figure emerged from the dark hallway.

Gloria blinked, trying to bring it into focus. Whoever it was moved very slowly and quietly. She couldn't see the face or enough of the body to tell much of anything. Except that it wasn't either of her grandchildren. Except that it was coming closer, steadily closer.

Slowly approaching her.

The figure passed an open doorway, wading through a pale stream of moonlight. Gloria recognized the sweater first, then the braided bun of gray hair. What she saw was impossible. She was so afraid she couldn't move. The fig-

148

ure moved closer, through the silver half-light of the hall-way.

It was the one person Gloria didn't want to see.

"Am I going crazy?" she thought wildly.

She'd seen quite enough of Nana when the old woman had been alive. Gloria had been forced to spend forty years of her married life in a polite cold war with that woman, sharing every holiday with her, picking her up every Sunday, including her in all of their plans. Year after year, she had been locked in a constant, silent battle with Nana, trying to justify her existence as the wife of Lou Rossi.

Nana had refused to let go of her son, Lou, for as long as she was alive. Only death had managed to pry loose her smothering, maternal grip. Now that she was finally gone, Gloria wanted her mother-in-law to stay dead. Not for her to be approaching down the hallway.

"Get away from me," whispered Gloria. "Haven't you done enough? Lou's mine now."

The shadowy figure seemed to know exactly what was in Gloria's heart. The shuddering image of the old woman began to wail, a terrible, echoing sound. The wail of a grieving mother for her child. Gloria covered her ears.

"I won't put up with it anymore," she cried. "You've taken all you're going to get. He's mine!"

The old woman seemed to be sobbing the same word over and over. An Italian word that Gloria had never heard before. Her tears made the word incomprehensible.

Nana reached out for her.

Gloria collapsed into merciful blackness.

5
"What Have You Done with Him?"

Aunt Jo was sound asleep.

She was the only one in the house who had achieved a state of peace. The remaining family members — Gina, her father, her stepmother, and her Grandpa — had quietly abandoned Aunt Jo to her slumbers and banded together in the living room by the cheerful, sparkling lights of the Christmas tree.

"Your Grandma shouldn't be interfering," said Grandpa. It wasn't that he really minded. He couldn't stop her, even if he did. He just wanted to know where she was, and that she was safe.

Gina was pacing back and forth. "Aaron's taking such a long time at the store."

"Where can Wally be?" said Barbara. She looked around, and scowled. "Where's Uncle Tony?"

"He's still upstairs," said Gina.

"Oh, fine," said Barbara. "So both Wally and Uncle Tony are missing. Both of them. And I'm not supposed to worry?"

"Rachel is upstairs, too," said Gina. "Why aren't you worrying about Rachel?"

"Rachel isn't a boy."

"That's not fair," said Gina curtly.

Barbara turned sharply to face her, caught off-guard by her step-daughter's criticism. "It's not a fair world," she snapped. "And I doubt if you know much about it."

"I know enough to trust my uncle," said Gina defiantly. "Your problem is you don't know who to trust."

"My problem!" Barbara's cheeks flushed with anger.

"So you trust your Uncle Tony?" interrupted Sam. "Well, I'm glad someone does."

"That will do," said Grandpa. He said it quietly, with authority. "Fighting among ourselves isn't going to help anything. Now, don't anyone leave. Something about this whole night is wrong. It's time I took a hand."

"Grandpa, where do you think you're going?" objected Gina. Her voice cracked. She was rapidly becoming so confused with guilt she could hardly speak. How much longer could she remain quiet about what was happening in that house? How many more family members could she allow to endanger themselves? To wander off on their own? "Now, you get back here. You have no business—"

"No, no, no," said Lou wearily. "Gina, honey, you listen to me. I guess I've always had a weird feeling about you moving into this place. I know more about this house than you do. I can't pretend I don't feel it anymore. Mom is still here. Some part of her never left. So, now do you see? If my mother is trapped in this house, she needs her son. And I've got a wife in this house who needs her husband."

He walked out of the living-room toward the stairs.

*

At first they thought it was Grandpa coming back.

Without warning, Uncle Tony appeared in the living room doorway. His clothes were in disarray, shirttail untucked. He looked like he'd just been in a fight.

"Well, look who's here," said Barbara.

She had risen to her feet in anticipation, as had her husband and Gina.

"Hello, everyone," said Uncle Tony.

"And where is my son, if you don't mind my asking?" Barbara flung the question at him like an accusation.

"Where's Wally?" repeated Uncle Tony stupidly. A nervous twitch of his eyes convinced her that he knew perfectly well.

"What have you done with him?"

Uncle Tony looked guilty. "Done?"

"Stop acting like you don't know what I'm talking about," cried Barbara, on the edge of tears.

"You leave Uncle Tony alone," objected Gina forcefully.

"Stay out of this, Gina," said her father. "Your dear uncle has had everyone in this family confused and worried long enough." Sam Rossi set down his wet shoes by the Christmas tree and faced his brother in his stocking feet. "I think it's time my brother and I had a few words with each other."

"You can have a chat somewhere else," said Gina, stepping between them.

Sam quickly, decisively, swept her to one side. "This is between your uncle and me, Gina," he said grimly. "I just want to ask my brother a few questions."

"Don't you even think about getting unpleasant," she said sternly. "Not in this house. I refuse to allow it."

"Just watch how you talk to me, young lady," said Sam. "I'm still your father."

"And I'm an adult," said Gina, "and this is my house and you're my guest."

Father and daughter faced each other.

"I'll tell you what I'm going to do," said Sam quietly. "I'm going upstairs to get my son. I'm going to ask him exactly what's been going on. And if it's what I think—" His eyes locked with those of his brother. "— then your dear Uncle Tony had better stay far, far away from me, as far as he can get."

His face flushed with barely suppressed emotion, Sam walked straight across the room and out the door. His stern, impatient footsteps hammered a determined staccato up the stairs, footsteps that echoed through the house. A moment later his voice rang through the hallway above them, in a call that was more like a demand, an angry shout.

"Wally—!"

6
What Uncle Tony Did

Barbara glared at Uncle Tony. "What have you done with my son?" she repeated. She might have said it again, if she hadn't seen Wally step out of the hall.

"If there's one person you don't have to worry about," said Wally, "it's Uncle Tony."

"Wally!" exclaimed Barbara, staring at her son. She grabbed him. She clutched him. "Where have you been?"

Wally sighed. He glanced sideways at Uncle Tony, and then reluctantly continued. "If you must know, I was upstairs searching the bathroom floor, just in case anything fell out before Uncle Tony took matters into his own hands."

"He did what?" Barbara gasped, unable to believe her ears. "Wally, honey, tell me exactly what he did."

"Uncle Tony caught me smoking—"

"Drugs!" cried Barbara. "He gave you drugs?"

152

"No, Mom," said Wally. "He took away my drugs. He gave me a lecture."

"A what?"

"A very boring lecture about the value of parents and family and sort of basic holiday stuff."

"But what did he do to you?" insisted his mother.

"He forced me over to the toilet."

"He did what?" Her voice rose, breaking.

"He made me dump my stuff in the toilet bowl."

For several stunned moments, no one could say anything.

"In the toilet bowl?" echoed Barbara numbly. She turned to Tony. "I thought you were the liberal one, the one who was so gung-ho on legalization?"

"There's a time for everything," qualified Tony. "And you're right, except that, well — I know this sounds strange, coming from me — but Christmas Eve, that's a time to be together with your family, not hiding in an upstairs closet."

"I wasn't hiding," said Wally.

Barbara finally spoke. Her words rang hollowly in the hushed living room. "I owe you an apology, Tony," she said. She turned to her son, cornering him with a single fierce glance. "As for you, mister, I don't care what your uncle says, if I ever catch you smoking that stuff again—"

"All right, all right."

"Do you hear what I'm saying?"

"I hear you. Besides, I already promised Uncle Tony."

Barbara had reached her limit. "You what?" She turned toward Uncle Tony and burst into tears. "I'm sorry. I've been awful to you. It's just that — I love my kids so much. It's so easy for bad things to happen. I couldn't bear it if anything bad happened to my kids."

Before she realized what he was doing, Uncle Tony took her in his arms, cautiously embracing the sister-in-law who had distrusted him for so long. "I love your kids, too. Not as much as you do, maybe — nobody loves them as much as their mother — but a lot. So, let's both love them, okay? And now I've got to go back upstairs. She's still here. She's trapped here, just like we are."

"Who are you talking about?" asked Barbara nervously. "All of a sudden, you're not making sense."

"I'm talking about Nana," said Tony. "She's here, and she's so unhappy. I don't know what's upset her. We need to find out, before things get any worse."

"No, Uncle Tony, don't," said Gina.

"I've got to, honey."

"But it's not safe. This whole house—" She wanted to tell him about running footsteps and red rubber balls, about how people could go to change a fuse and never come back.

"I won't be long," said her uncle. "I promise."

"I'm going with you," said Gina, and she would have, too. Except that just as her uncle opened the staircase door, she heard something else from another direction altogether.

A noise from downstairs.

Was it banging? Was it a voice?

Aaron. Who else could it be? He was trying to call her. He needed her. But he wasn't down there. No one was down there.

He had to be!

Gina ran toward the basement stairs.

7
The Good Father

Sam Rossi didn't like being helpless. He could only twiddle his thumbs for so long and then it was time to step in and take over. His exasperation with waiting for other people to solve his problems betrayed itself in the angry energy surging through his body. He lunged up the stairs.

"Wally," he called. "Wally, come here. Right now."

No answer.

The west hall was still familiar from childhood. He'd played in those rooms as a boy. He knew the layout of each, and hunted quickly through them, closets and all. No sign of him. He shouted his son's name.

No answer.

What had happened? Once they were going to be the Great All-American Family. For years, it seemed like everything would work out perfectly. Three great kids. And now all three were heading straight for hell.

He heard the creak of a floorboard.

"Wally?" Sam snorted with exasperation. The kid was going to drive him crazy. He started down the east hall, just in time to see, through the open door of the far room, the shadow of someone moving back out of sight.

So, there he was.

"Okay, Wally, come on out. Let's not ruin Christmas Eve. I won't be mad, I promise. Wally—"

Sam approached the open doorway. The moment he stepped across the threshold, he saw someone slip back into the shadows, toward an open door at the back of the room.

"Wally," he said. "I'm trying to be patient. You're going to make me lose my temper. Don't push me, son. I don't understand why you want to make me angry."

Sam reached the door. His son was nowhere to be seen. The room opened into a huge closet. No Wally. He almost turned away, and then noticed yet another door at the far end of the closet, slightly open. Another door? It was almost too small to believe it really led anywhere—

At that moment, the door clicked shut.

Sam stared, and then grinned. "All right, mister, one last chance. Come out now, or take your chances."

Silence.

"You're pissing me off, Wally."

Sam grabbed the little door, and tried to jerk it open. It wouldn't budge. "Wally, I'm warning you." He rattled it furiously, and in doing so discovered that it opened inward.

Into a narrow staircase. A staircase that reeked of marijuana. That kid! Now Sam was becoming furious. He pushed his way through the entrance. His shoulders bumped against the tight, crowding walls. He came to the top of the stairs, but there was nowhere to go. They seemed to just stop. Why build a staircase to nowhere?

"Stairs lead somewhere," muttered Sam Rossi. "It's a law of nature. They always do."

And somewhere up there, his son was blatantly defying him. He searched. He felt along the surface with his fingertips. A slight edge, a fine crack, framed a portion of the upper wall at the dead end of the passage.

The stairs did lead somewhere. They led to a somewhere currently blocked by an inserted wooden panel.

He managed to get his fingernails into the crack. He clawed at the edge of the panel. It moved. After several tries, he succeeded in shoving it to one side.

A dark, triangular-shaped emptiness slid open before him. He peered within. It was a third-floor attic tucked under the roof, musty and stale with disuse. At the far end was a small, dusty window, which admitted a shaft of gray light from the snow-white sky.

What in the world had he found?

Clearly, from the look of it, a space which none of the previous tenants had discovered. He peered into the shadowy depths, trying to detect a hint of movement to reveal the hiding place of his son.

"Wally?"

Nothing moved. Sam wasn't satisfied. The kid had to be there somewhere. He scrambled up over the edge.

He was at once covered in dust. It swirled around him as he got to his feet. Squinting to keep it out of his eyes, he brushed himself off. "I'll bet Gina doesn't even know about this," he thought. "It must run the length of the whole house." He looked forward to being able to tell his daughter about an unknown feature of her own home.

But where was Wally hiding? How far back did it go? He'd be able to see more by the small window. Ducking down his head to make his way, he braced himself against the exposed ceiling joists, half-crouching as he crossed the attic. Dust surged and eddied around his shoes.

A shadow shifted on the wall. He turned around, peering into the darkness. Someone was silhouetted in the entrance of the attic, standing very, very still. Clever. How did Wally get behind him?

"Did I find your little hiding-place?" said Sam. "Not bad. Okay, Wally, time to straighten up."

Silence.

"Are you pouting?" said Sam, his irritation bristling. "Or are you just stoned?"

Silence.

Anger rippled through Sam. He forced himself to remain still, to remain calm. This was no time for emotion.

"Are you determined to ruin our Christmas Eve?"

Silence.

It suddenly occurred to Sam, on the edge of blowing his cool completely, that the defiant figure in the shadows of the attic might not be the child he assumed. Rachel! Why, that little—! And, of course, she would enjoy testing her father's patience to the very limit.

"Rachel, if that's you," said Sam, "if you have been standing there making fun of your father, mocking me, you're playing with fire. And I mean it."

Silence.

"Answer me this minute!"

Silence.

Sam lost it. Kids could be so selfish, so ungrateful, so infuriating! Someone had to teach them a lesson. He took one angry stride forward. That was all the farther he got. Then the figure stepped out of the shadows enough for him to see that it wasn't Rachel or Wally.

He tried to scream.

8
The Good Daughter

Did she hear something, or not?

Rachel wasn't sure about anything anymore and that's what she hated most. Had she gotten high from breathing her brother's marijuana smoke? She hoped the smell wasn't clinging to her clothes. Was she starting to hear things now? She didn't know what to think. All she knew was that she hated it here at Nana's house. She wished that Christmas was over.

After Uncle Tony flushed her brother's stash down the toilet and that whole dramatic scene, which she had thoroughly enjoyed, Rachel had locked herself into the upstairs bathroom.

At last! You knew where you were in a bathroom. A bathroom was reality. A bathroom was safe. Then she remembered that it was here, in that very bathroom, that Aunt Jo had seen whatever Aunt Jo had seen. Which, of course, ruined everything. How can you relax when you're listening to every creak and scratch?

It could have been just the wind outside, the snowstorm shrieking against the house, whistling through every crack. Her ears were playing tricks on her. She was freaking out. Then the wind died down, the snowstorm hushed, and she heard it again. From somewhere upstairs.

"Oh, my God," thought Rachel bleakly. "Somebody's screaming." She was so scared, she could hardly move. "Doesn't anybody else hear it? Why doesn't somebody do something? Where's my Dad when you need him?"

She had been sitting on the toilet seat, staring down into the reassuring patterns of the black and white floor tiles, hugging herself. Now she rose, walked nervously to the door, and forced herself to touch the cold doorknob.

Another muted scream. But this time with a terrible difference. This time she recognized the urgent voice that was shouting in the walls. It was the voice of her father.

In all her life, she had never heard him sound so needy, so vulnerable. She didn't hesitate a moment longer. She didn't stop to think about danger. She flung open the bathroom door, rushed out into the hall, and looked about in all directions, listening for the slightest sound or clue.

There it was again.

Her father's voice. It seemed to come from the end of the hall. From the last guest room. She bolted through the open door, across the floorboards, through the huge closet, through the small door at the end, and into the narrow staircase. It reeked from her brother's secret puffing. Up the stairs. But something was different now. The stairs didn't abruptly stop. They opened up into a big, dark emptiness.

Not quite empty. Someone was cowering in the far corner.

"Dad?"

She swung herself easily, confidently up into the attic. It was filthy, like some kind of tomb. There he was, doubled over on the floor, making a strange, choking sound.

She worked her way closer, through the uncertain footing. She realized he was crying. She didn't think twice. She clutched him in her arms. She held her father, her father!

"What happened, Dad? Tell me, tell me. What?"

He mumbled something.

"I can't understand you. Talk slower. What happened?"

"I don't know what happened." That was all Sam Rossi could say, at first. "I don't know what I saw. I don't know what I believe. About anything. But I know one thing. I know that I love you, Rachel. I love you so much."

9
Wife and Mother

"Gloria?"

Lou was halfway down the other hall before he glimpsed her through an open doorway, stretched out on the floor. Something in his chest lurched so violently at the sight that he was sure his seventy-plus heart was calling it quits.

That didn't slow him down from rushing to her side.

"Gloria—"

She opened her eyes. When she recognized his face bending over her, she wrapped her arms around his neck. "It was her, Lou." She spoke weakly, but the words were perfectly clear. "I saw her. Your mother. She's here."

He held his wife in his arms.

"Take it easy. I know, I know. I was afraid of that. I don't think she can leave." He gently stroked his wife's hair. He held her. He heard Sam calling his kids. He heard passing footsteps in the hall. None of that mattered. As long as Gloria was all right, safe in his arms, the situation was under control.

Neither of them noticed the figure in the doorway. They didn't look up until they heard Tony sigh with relief.

"Mom, Dad!" he exclaimed. "So it's you in here. I heard something, and I thought — well, I was afraid that—" He would have finished, but he began to realize what he was seeing in front of him. "Mom, are you all right?"

"It's okay," said Lou, "she's fine."

"But you're both on the floor."

He was still trying to calm down Tony when his other son appeared, led by his daughter, Rachel, both covered in grime. Sam's face was filthy and streaked with tears, but his arm was around Rachel's shoulders.

"Grandma, are you okay?" cried Rachel.

Footsteps echoed up the staircase from the first floor, and down the second-floor hallway toward them. The sounds became Barbara and Wally.

"Grandma?" gasped Wally, stopping abruptly in his tracks.

Before Barbara could cry out at the sight of Gloria on the floor, Lou held up a reassuring hand.

"She's fine," said Lou. "Really. No need to worry. Even your Grandma gets winded once in a while. She's just had a little too much excitement for one night."

"So have we all," said Barbara.

She took a second look at her husband and daughter, both of them smeared with filth, holding hands. Not until then did Barbara realize that she had, for some time now, been clutching the hand of Wally.

She looked at Sam. Sam looked at her. They both realized at the same time who was missing.

"Where's Gina?"

CHAPTER FOURTEEN

Buried Alive

1
The Other Side

Alert for the slightest sound, Gina descended the staircase and crossed the empty basement. She stopped at the foot of the wooden stairs leading up to the cantina door.

"Aaron?" whispered Gina.

She thought she heard muffled rustling.

"Aaron, is that you?"

She stepped into the small, damp enclosure. Something loomed before her face like a shrunken head. She batted it away. The lightbulb swung wildly dangling on its string. She flicked the light switch. The bulb flared, flickered. Barely enough light, but enough.

The cantina smelled of earth and old, wooden boards. Aaron was not there, that much was certain. Just two big wine barrels, and the ancient fuse box, and walls lined with planks of shelving.

Gina took a step inside, another step. Then she turned around and used the whisk broom to brace open the cantina door. Listening for the slightest sound, she noticed something on the ground.

A mouse, its neck broken by a trap, curled up into a lifeless, wet fur ball. She shuddered, backed away from it, and looked again. Not a dead mouse. A soaked, balled-up stocking. Aaron's stocking.

She picked up the sopping wad of wool in quiet panic, her imagination scrambling desperately for an explanation.

Then she saw something else on the floor, lying between the large wooden barrels.

Aaron's flashlight.

What was it doing down there? She squatted and stretched out her arm between the two barrels. Just out of reach. Grabbing the bottom shelf, she braced herself to stretch farther. Her fingers managed to close around the flashlight. The moment she switched on its beam, however, the wall abruptly collapsed under her weight.

What had looked like a wall slid away from her, and swung open. With a cry, Gina fell through.

She landed on a body.

She screamed.

She was still screaming as the concealed door slid shut behind her, closing her into an inky darkness. A darkness that would have swallowed her, had it not been for the leaping, rolling ray of the flashlight. The beam lurched and ricocheted over the walls. Then the light lanced downward, onto a face.

It was Aaron. He lay under a thick, old plank of wood that appeared to be a fallen shelf from the other side of the fake wall. His face was pale gray, his forehead caked with dried blood. His rain jacket was spread out beneath him like a dirty, wrinkled plastic tarp. He moaned. She became frantic, but managed to retain her presence of mind long enough to prop up the flashlight and drag the fallen shelf off of him. He groaned.

"Careful. Don't move."

He moved, slowly, cautiously.

"Oh, Aaron, Aaron, are you all right?"

"Maybe not all right, but I'm alive," he said. "I don't think anything's broken."

"Your head looks broken," she said. "This old plank must have whacked you a good one."

"I think they all took turns."

"But I've found you."

"What's left of me."

She covered his mouth with wild, insane kisses. "I was so worried I was half out of my mind." She was crying and

162

laughing at the same time. "I love you so much. I was so afraid." She suddenly stopped kissing him. "You could be seriously hurt. Something could be broken."

"Nothing broken that wasn't broken before. My head feels like it's just barely holding the pieces together." He squinted blindly into the surrounding darkness. "Where exactly am I?"

"On the other side of the cantina, behind the wine barrels." She peered into the blackness, poking at it with the flashlight beam. "For some reason, there's a secret little room."

The room was not only secret, but filthy with disuse. The cobwebs alone were proof that it hadn't been touched in years. It wasn't large, just wide enough for Aaron to be stretched across a crude dirt floor.

Aiming the flashlight, Gina took a step beyond Aaron. That was all it took for the beam of light to reveal the room's purpose.

Hanging on the wall, beneath a carved wooden crucifix, was a framed, old-fashioned photograph of a very young child. A smiling little boy was looking at the camera. He was flanked by several smaller photos. All pictures of the same dark-haired, dark-eyed little boy.

"That face," said Aaron. "I've seen that kid before." At first he couldn't remember where. Then it hit him. "The day I fell off the ladder. That's him. That's who I saw in the window."

Boxes of children's clothes. Toys. Marbles Stuffed animals.

An old wooden crib with rockers was the centerpiece of the buried shrine. It was painted with laughing clown faces and bright circus stripes. The initials "V.A.R." were elaborately engraved over the headboard.

A wooden plaque hung above the framed photograph and the crib. The name engraved across it was Vito Angelo Rossi. Beneath the name was carved 3 February 1918 - 24 December 1919.

"That's it," said Gina. "That's the word. Vito."

"What did you say?"

"That's what she was saying," said Gina, "over and over again. Vito. Vito."

And now Gina knew why.

Grandpa had not been Nana's only son. He had been her only living son. Her only surviving son. That's why Nana could never stop clinging to Grandpa. Because her first son, her little Vito, had been cruelly snatched away.

2
In the Garden

Flashlight in hand, they slid open the secret door from the inside. She supported his weight, with one of her arms wrapped around him. "Just up this one step. Lean on me." With the flashlight beam leading the way, she helped Aaron back into the cantina. Propping him up against one of the wine barrels, Gina swatted at his ruined clothes, brushing off the dirt and dust and dried blood that covered him.

"You look disgusting," she said.

"You're not exactly spotless yourself."

Then she noticed that the door of the cantina was closed.

"I thought I propped that open. Where's that whisk broom? Stay here, don't move."

She crossed the cantina in a few quick, nervous strides, and pushed open the small door. It swung out into the dark basement. She meant to simply re-brace the door with the fallen whisk broom, and then return to help Aaron. From the moment she opened the cantina door, she never looked back.

The basement door on the far side of the room blew suddenly open. It clattered against the wall. A howling gust of wind and snow rushed inside. From the open door, from the snowy confusion of the night, came the sound of a child crying.

She could just barely hear it. The moment she did, she stopped hearing everything else.

"Gina, what is it?" called Aaron from inside the cantina.

She didn't hear his question. She had forgotten all about him. Descending the three stairs out of the cantina, she headed across the snow-invaded basement toward the open door and the roaring whiteness of the night.

"Gina, where are you going?" called a voice behind her, but the words had no more effect on her than the snow blowing in her face which she didn't feel.

She had crossed the basement and was almost at the door when the shovel propped against the wall, entangled with a rake and broom and other gardening equipment, suddenly toppled forward and clattered on the floor at her feet. Gina didn't find it surprising at all. She simply bent down, grabbed the shovel by the handle, and took it along with her. With no thought of the cold, she walked out the basement door.

"Gina, come back!"

But the words echoing behind her hardly mattered. What mattered was the child crying. What mattered was the square of whiteness before her, outlined by stark, leafless beanpoles and the snow-covered raspberry briar. What mattered was dragging the shovel behind her, toward what was waiting for her in the vegetable patch. She stopped.

"Gina—!"

Something about that corner of the garden.

She gripped the handle of the shovel with both hands. It sliced downward into the frozen white blanket covering the earth. It shouldn't have cut through the frigid ground so easily. Again and again she drove it down, upturning chunks of winter-hardened soil. In the midst of the snowstorm, she was digging a hole. The ground was hard with ice, but her shovel possessed a strength far beyond her. By the time Aaron hobbled up to her, rain jacket flapping behind him, and dragged the shovel out of her hands, she had uncovered one corner of an old wooden box.

"Gina, stop!"

"There it is!" she cried. "That's it, Aaron. That's what it's all about. Can't you feel it? All the trouble comes from here. It's the same place I was digging the night I sleepwalked, the same place! Give me back the shovel."

"Stop it, Gina, let go."

She didn't wait for the shovel, or anything else. She fell to her knees in the whiteness, pawing away the remaining snow and earth with numb, bloodless fingers.

"Gina, stop—!"

She clawed open the lid. The rotting wood crumbled in her hands. The stench of death.

Bones.

And a red rubber ball.

3
No More Secrets

Lou held his wife in his arms, surrounded by the concerned members of his family. The only grandchild not accounted for now opened the door below them.

Wet with snow, red-cheeked with the cold, Gina quickly ascended the staircase to the upper floor, followed at a slower but urgent hobble by her long absent boyfriend, his forehead caked with blood. They hurried toward the others.

"What happened?" cried Barbara anxiously, but Gina interrupted her.

"Grandpa," she said. "In the garden— Something just led me — I mean, I walked right to it. I just started digging, and I found a box. And Grandpa, inside it — inside it are bones."

Lou was the only one who didn't gasp in horror and amazement. He sighed.

"You knew about it?"

"Aunt Jo is right," he said. "Too many secrets in this family. You need to know the truth."

"Know what?" said Gina. "Know about Nana's other son? Know about your brother, Grandpa?"

Lou winced. "Yes, that's what I mean. About what happened to Vito. And to Nana."

It had been painful enough keeping it hidden in his heart. The time had come to tell.

"I never knew my brother," said Lou. "Mom and Dad never talked about him. He was just a big, painful silence that happened before I came along. One of the last things my Dad did before I joined the Navy was to tell me about Vito. To tell me how he died.

"It happened on Christmas Eve. He wasn't quite two years old. He had been a total pest all day, according to my father, a terrible little troublemaker with his rubber ball. Bouncing it all over the place. Getting in my mother's way. He broke one of her favorite vases. Then he caused her to burn a batch of Christmas cookies. She had to open all the windows — and it was cold! — to let the smoke out of the house.

"Your Nana had left him alone just long enough to take something out of the oven. Nobody knows for sure what happened. Vito was playing in the hall. His ball must have bounced into the bedroom, and out the open window. They found it afterward in the garden.

"When my mother finally tracked him down, she found Vito up on the bedroom windowsill, hanging over the edge, trying to see where his ball went. She was so shocked and scared for his safety that she screamed. Her scream — he lost his balance and fell. His head hit one of the two cement stairs leading down to the basement door. My mother never stopped blaming herself."

A hush settled over them all.

"How awful!" said Gina. "Then the bones in the garden—"

"In those days," said Lou, "immigrants sometimes did things their own way. The codes weren't so strict. My father said it was impossible to get the dead kid out of her arms. She went sort of crazy. He let her bury him out back."

"Not much of a burial place for a baby," said Sam. "A vegetable patch isn't exactly consecrated ground."

"Maybe that's the problem," said Gina. "Maybe it just seemed like a good solution at the time."

"Maybe that's why something led you right to the spot where those bones were buried," said Aaron.

"I think we should do Nana a favor," said her father. "Let's give the kid a decent resting-place."

Impulsively, Gina reached out and squeezed her father's hand. "I think Nana would like that very much. I think that's what Nana wants more than anything."

"Is losing her baby why Nana went crazy?" asked Wally.

"That happened before I was born," said Lou. "Everyone thought she had gotten over it. It wasn't until years later, near the very end, that Vito started coming up more and more. She couldn't remember where she left her knitting needles five minutes ago, but she couldn't forget Vito. She became obsessed with the idea that he was still here. That she had misplaced him somewhere in the house. Sometimes, when I stopped by after work, I would find her all worked up, going from room to room, calling a little boy who had been dead for over seventy years.

"It got worse.

"One day downtown, my mother came across some little toddler wandering in a department store. She thought she had finally found her Vito. She walked right out of the store with him. Fortunately, she was stopped by the store detectives. They phoned me out at the real estate office. I had to go get her. The parents were so happy to have their kid back, they didn't press charges. That same day I made arrangements with a nursing home.

"I didn't have any choice.

"I tried to tell her she'd be moving. That was when she started hiding from me. Usually I could find her in one of the rooms. The hardest place to find her was in the attic."

"In the where?" interrupted Gina.

"The closet at the end of the east hall has a little staircase," he began, but again she cut him off.

"Yes, I found it!" said Gina. "But it goes nowhere."

"It doesn't go nowhere," interrupted her father, Sam. "I can tell you from experience that it very definitely goes somewhere. It leads to an attic over the second floor. Somebody sealed it off with a panel of wood."

"I'm the one who sealed it off," said Lou. "That's why I never mentioned it. I never wanted to see it again. I fought with her up there, my desperate, crazy mother. I was sick of dragging her out of there. So I boarded it up.

"The day she discovered that it was walled off, she went out of control. Running from room to room. Not making sense. Kicking and struggling, pulling away from me. She was frantic to find Vito. She kept calling for him, and hiding from me, and crying when I found her. Then before I realized what she was doing, she got away from me and ran over to the window, the same window that Vito — and she just—"

4
"It's Her!"

Lou looked up. Just beyond Gina and Aaron in the doorway, he could see someone standing in the hall. The figure was blurry and slightly faded, but there was no doubt who it was.

"Lou, it's her!" whispered Gloria, clawing at his arm.

Gina spun around and gasped, stumbling backward into Aaron's arms, unable to turn away from the still, shadowy form.

Rachel screamed. Sam drew his daughter to him, held her against him while he stared.

Nana was wearing the pink sweater she had knitted herself. Her indestructible old apron from the produce stand on Beacon Avenue was tied around her waist. Her hair, streaked with gray, was tightly coiled into a bun.

Her face began to contort. Her mouth twisted open in unbearable grief. Before Lou could move to comfort her, he saw his older son, Tony, step forward.

"Nana—" he stammered bravely.

She cried out, her voice echoing with a wall-rattling pain. She clawed at her hair, tearing apart the neat coils of the bun, leaving her long gray locks wild and scattered.

Tony stumbled backward in sheer terror, tripped over his own feet, and fell sprawling on the floor.

She didn't seem to see her favorite grandson. What was left of Nana was in terrible pain. She gave another cry. An icy wind surged around her.

The sound of his mother's voice cut through Lou like jagged glass. As she cried out again, he clambered up onto his feet and helped Gloria rise beside him.

A shuffling rush of footsteps.

She was gone. His mother had suddenly disappeared from the hallway, fleeing into one of the far rooms.

Lou forced himself to follow her. Pushing through the stunned members of his family, past Gina and Aaron, he walked down the hall to the doorway. Gloria was right beside him. Gina and Aaron weren't far behind.

Another pattering of footfalls.

She was little more than a darker darkness in the undefined shadows of the far corner. He stepped closer, his wife pressed to his side, clutching him.

"Mother—"

The foggy image turned to face him. Dead eyes from the past seemed to stare straight through him, eyes harrowed by pain.

"Mom, we want to help you," he said. "I know how unhappy you are."

Her wail rang down the hallway.

"I had no choice, Mom!" he cried. "You couldn't take care of yourself. I had to do what I thought was best."

That was when Gina stepped forward. Aaron grabbed at her arm, trying to stop her, but she pulled away from him.

"Nana, please—" she said, stepping toward her, trying not to shake as she felt the icy chill. "We're your family. We're your children. You should love us. Give us your love, Nana — and I promise — I promise to give your dear Vito a real resting place—"

An otherworldly chill seemed to pass straight through Gina. She didn't understand what had happened until she detected a small, rippling distortion hurtling toward the

170

image of Nana. A child's squeal of recognition. A mother's sob of joy. Nana was suddenly clutching her lost Vito in her arms, a bundle of arms and legs and laughter.

A shriek of pure release rang through the halls and rooms of Nana's house. The blurry figures seemed to become one, to disintegrate, collapse, dissolving into the shadows.

Gina's knees might have buckled out from under her if Aaron hadn't come up beside her.

Grandpa took his wife into his arms. Grandma was crying.

"Now, you stop that," he said to her. "You're fine and so am I." Lou held her warmly against his heart. "This whole family is fine. Better than we've been in a long time."

CHAPTER FIFTEEN

Christmas Morning

1
The Last Dream

"Gina—!"

A voice so far away, she can hardly hear it.

Suddenly she's running. She obeys at once. She always obeys that voice. The world is bright with sunshine and she's five years old and flowers are bursting open on every side, huge blossoms exploding with color, as she runs through the gardens toward Nana's voice. She scampers down the sloping green lawn toward the leafy beanpoles and tall sunflowers peeking over the raspberry briar, toward the old woman standing in the crowded green rows of vegetables.

"Gina," she calls. "I've got something to show you."

She hurries as fast as she can, her little feet pattering down the rain-warped planks that crisscross the garden as walking paths.

"I want you to know all my secrets," says Nana. "All the secrets of my garden—"

Gina gets closer and closer, and is just about to see what Nana is waiting to show her when she discovers that she isn't running anymore.

She has gotten bigger and the garden has gotten smaller and Nana is no longer calling. Nana is gone. Gina is the one who is calling, "Vito! Vito—!"

Someone is running toward her. A little figure moving through the leafy rows. She can hear a child's excited peal

173

of laughter, a squeal of innocent glee. She is kneeling in the garden, and opening her arms.

"Come here, Vito," she whispers. "Vito—!"

2
First Light

Two churches in the neighborhood were stubborn enough and old-fashioned enough to ring in the morning with a joyful tolling and bonging. The bells woke her.

Gina opened her eyes. It was Christmas Day.

She blinked. Then the whole night came back to her in a rush. The most frightening night of her life! And yet this morning, somehow, everything seemed different. Aaron was still asleep. She slid out from under his arm, and padded barefoot across the cold, wooden floor to the window.

Outside, beyond the whitened vegetable garden, lay a stunned, snowbound city. The sky was a pure, clear winter blue. Without a single tumbling flake.

The snow had finally stopped falling.

Car wheels girded in chains had already begun clanking and grinding the street into a drivable slush. As she watched, one early, intrepid bus grumbled bravely down Beacon Avenue. She hurried back to her warm bed and electric blanket. She could hear voices down the hall in the kitchen, the smells of coffee and bacon.

The smells of reality. The night before had been filled with so many shocks and surprises that the world seemed strange and new. Had it all really happened? The secret room in the cantina? The discovery in the garden? An actual ghost, right there before them all!

A very concrete fact sprawled peacefully beside her, half out of the tangled covers, softly snoring. Her Aaron was safe with her in bed. She didn't move for a while, just watched him breathe.

She placed the palm of her hand on her own warm, flat belly. Somewhere under her fingertips, a seed was stirring

174

with life, a seed planted by the man beside her, the man she loved, right there on the hard, wooden floor of their bedroom on Halloween night.

Gina thought about the baby and Aaron, about the dream and everything that had happened the night before. She cried so quietly that Aaron never heard her. She whispered, "Yes, Nana, I promise."

She kissed him awake. "Merry Christmas." He mumbled something incoherent and nuzzled up against her. "How's your poor head?"

"Hurts," he said.

"Would a kiss make it feel better?"

"Yes, please."

She applied the appropriate medicine. "I'd like to spend all morning right here with you," she said. "But we have a houseful of guests."

"Our guests can wait a few more minutes," said Aaron. "You and I have to talk."

3
The Child

Rachel was the first one to leave her room. Dressed in her sister's pajamas, she bravely ventured downstairs, turned on the kitchen lights, located coffee beans and a grinder, and got the coffeemaker gurgling cheerfully.

"Need any help?"

Her father stood in the doorway, in a T-shirt and sweatpants borrowed from Aaron.

"Merry Christmas," said Rachel. "Think you're up to making toast?"

"I think I can handle toast," said Sam. "Any special instructions?"

"Easy on the butter."

When Barbara came down, she found her husband and daughter making coffee and toast together. A miracle! She gave them each a kiss on the cheek, a "Merry Christmas," and busied herself on the other side of the kitchen making orange juice.

They didn't realize Wally had joined them until they heard him in the corner, snickering as he sketched them, transforming them into a busy family of cartoon beavers.

Rachel took a look, snorted, and hit him on the head.

"And who's that supposed to be?" said Uncle Tony, grinning over his nephew's shoulder. "A bald beaver."

The moment he saw Tony in the kitchen, Sam put down the butter knife, crossed the room in three strides, and embraced his brother. "Merry Christmas," he said. "I hope you can forget all the ugly things I said last night."

"What things?" said Tony. He returned the hug. "Merry Christmas, little brother."

Barbara took a curious peek in her son's sketchbook. To her surprise, she burst out laughing. "Is that supposed to be me?" Her surprise doubled when Wally gave her a peck on the cheek.

"Merry Christmas, Mom," he muttered, intently returning to work in his sketchbook.

Her son had kissed her!

"Looks like we slept in," said Grandpa, as he and Grandma entered the kitchen.

"Not as late as our hostess," said Rachel. The door to Gina and Aaron's room was still closed.

"Let them sleep," said Grandma. "Come on, Lou, let's get some breakfast going. See if there's any bacon. I'll make scrambled eggs."

"I certainly hope the phone is working by now."

Grumpy but relieved to be back on her feet, Aunt Jo made her way to the breakfast nook, one hand pressed to her forehead. She at once dismissed the onslaught of questions.

"I don't want to talk about it," she said, with a disdainful wave. "I've got a splitting headache. What a miserable night. That horrible wine. And that bed! I have never been so uncomfortable in my life. You couldn't pay me to spend another hour in this dreadful house. Where's the coffee?" She was clearly feeling improved. "Just a bit of toast, dear," she said to Sam. "I think I'm ready to call for my cab. The sooner I get home where I belong, the better."

"Don't leave yet, Aunt Jo."

Gina and Aaron appeared in the kitchen doorway, both still in their bathrobes.

"We've got presents to open yet," said Gina. "And we have something to tell you." She turned to Aaron. "Do you want to tell them, or shall I?"

"Actually, I'd like to tell them," said Aaron. He regarded the surrounding circle of faces, unable to conceal his happiness. "We want you to be the first to know. Your wonderful Gina has agreed to be my wife."

The family converged on them. Gina and Aaron were engulfed in hugs and kisses, cries and laughter and tears of joy.

"And the baby?" said Rachel.

"I think Nana has made it pretty clear," said Gina, "that if we want to live in her house and remain in one piece, we had better present her with her first great-great-grandchild." Her father started to cry, and hugged her. Gina hugged him back. "Better get ready to be a grandfather."

"And just how are you two going to afford this baby?" asked Gloria bluntly.

"We'll do whatever we have to do," said Aaron. "We may have to cut a few corners. Medical school may have to wait."

"My first grandchild," said Sam. "Don't worry about medical school. You're one of us now. Money isn't going to be a problem." He chuckled. "It's going to be a boy. I'm sure of it."

"Dad!" groaned Rachel. "You'll never change."

"If it is a boy," said Gina, "then Aaron and I have already made a decision. His name will be Vito."

The lightbulb in the ceiling fixture exploded.

Aunt Jo screamed.

Bright, twinkling colors spilled toward them through the dining room arch. With gasps of alarm and concern, they abandoned breakfast and crowded toward the doorway. Winking and sparkling, all the Christmas tree lights had snapped on without anyone touching the switch.

"Something must be wrong with the lights again."

"But the electricity has been fine all morning."

Gina looked from one face to another of her family. No one wanted to say it out loud. Gina said it out loud.

"Nana always loved a beautiful Christmas tree."

"Nana has nothing to do with it," said Aunt Jo. "Your dear Nana isn't here to turn on your Christmas lights."

"Of course not," said Aaron, putting his arm around Gina, drawing her closer. "It's just a fault in the electrical system."

"That's all it is," said Gina. "You know these old houses."

*

Nick DiMartino has had 18 plays in full-run productions. His *Dracula* premiered at Seattle Children's Theatre in 1982, followed by his adaptations of *Pinocchio* and Hans Christian Andersen's *The Snow Queen*. His *Frankenstein* sold out in Honolulu, Nashville, Louisville, Dallas and Milwaukee. His plays include *Raven,* inspired by Pacific Northwest Indian legends, an authentic Arabic version of *Aladdin,* and a Grimms Brothers version of *Snow White*. He wrote three musicals for Bellevue Children's Theatre, including *Ozma of Oz.*

His four-woman Victorian vampire thriller, *The Red Forest,* won 2nd Place at the 1987 Pacific Northwest Writers Conference. His Italian farce, *Stop the Wedding!,* was a finalist in the 1988 New City Theater Playwrights Festival. His new version of *Babes in Toyland,* with the original music of Victor Herbert, was the 1994 opening production of the new Village Theatre in Issaquah.

Since 1970, he has been the book-buyer for the HUB Branch of the University Bookstore.

Buy Locally - Buy Independent

INDEPENDENT BOOKSELLERS OF WASHINGTON (IBOW) is an association of locally-owned bookstores committed to understanding and responding to the needs of the communities they serve. It is dedicated to providing continued education and training in the bookselling trade, supporting literacy programs, preventing censorship, and preserving the right to read.

A portion of the proceeds from the sale of this book will go toward supporting IBOW. Thanks to Pacific Pipeline for their help in this project.

MEMBER STORES

BAILEY-COY BOOKS
Seattle (206) 323-8842

BEKS BOOKSTORE
Seattle (206) 624-1328
(206) 224-7028

BETWEEN THE COVERS BOOKSHOP
Woodinville (206) 481-9117

EAGLE HARBOR BOOK COMPANY
Bainbridge Island (206) 842-5332

EDMONDS BOOKSHOP
Edmonds (206) 775-2789

ELLIOT BAY BOOK COMPANY
Seattle (206) 624-6600

FREMONT PLACE BOOK COMPANY
Seattle (206) 547-5970

HEALING PAGES BOOKSTORE
Seattle (206) 283-7621

ISLAND BOOKS
Mercer Island (206) 232-6920

LADY JAYNE'S BOOKS
Tacoma (206) 564-6168

LEFT BANK BOOK COLLECTIVE
Seattle (206) 622-0195

LINDON BOOKSTORE
Enumclaw (360) 825-1388

M. COY BOOKS, INC.
Seattle (206) 623-5354

MADISON PARK BOOKS
Seattle (206) 328-READ

MAGNOLIA'S BOOKSTORE
Seattle (206) 283-1062

NEW WOMAN BOOKS
Kent (206) 854-3487

PISTIL BOOKS AND NEWS
Seattle (206) 325-5401

PORT BOOK AND NEWS
Port Angeles (360) 452-6367

PORT GARDNER BAY BOOKS AND NEWS
Everett (206) 339-2626

PUSS 'N BOOKS
Redmond (206) 885-6828

QUEEN ANNE AVENUE BOOKS
Seattle (206) 283-5624

RED AND BLACK BOOKS
Seattle (206) 322-7323

SCOTT'S BOOKSTORE AND CARD SHOP
Mount Vernon (360) 336-6181

SECOND STORY BOOKSTORE
Seattle (206) 547-4605

SERAPHIM BOOKS AND GIFTS
Seattle (206) 932-4147

SNOW GOOSE BOOKSTORE
Stanwood (360) 629-3631

SQUARE ONE BOOKS
Seattle (206) 935-5764

TOTEM BOOK SHOP
Kirkland   (206) 821-4343
Monroe   (360) 794-0544

UNIVERSITY BOOK STORE
U. District   (206) 634-3400
Bellevue   (206) 632-9500
HUB   (206) 543-5896
South Campus/Medical   (206) 543-6582
Downtown Seattle   (206) 545-9230
Tacoma   (206) 272-8080

VILLAGE BOOKS
Bellingham (360) 671-2626

WATERMARK BOOK COMPANY
Anacortes (360) 293-4277

WIDE WORLD BOOKS AND MAPS
Seattle (206) 634-3453